Memoirs of a Novelist

Memoirs of a Novelist

Virginia Woolf

ET REMOTISSIMA PROPE

Modern Voices

Modern Voices
Published by Hesperus Press Limited
4 Rickett Street, London SW6 1RU
www.hesperuspress.com

First published in Great Britain in 1985 by The Hogarth Press
First published by Hesperus Press Limited, 2006

Text by Virginia Woolf © Quentin Bell, Angelica Garnett and Julian Bell
1917, 1919, 1921, 1923, 1942, 1944, 1973, 1977, 1985
The Estate of Virginia Woolf asserts the moral right of Virginia Woolf
to be identified as the Author of the text of *Memoirs of a Novelist*.

Designed and typeset by Fraser Muggeridge studio
Printed in Jordan by the Jordan National Press

ISBN: 1-84391-423-9
ISBN13: 978-1-84391-423-5

All rights reserved. This book is sold subject to the condition that it shall not be
resold, lent, hired out or otherwise circulated without the express prior consent
of the publisher.

Contents

Phyllis and Rosamond

In this very curious age, when we are beginning to require pictures of people, their minds and their coats, a faithful outline, drawn with no skill but veracity, may possibly have some value.

Let each man, I heard it said the other day, write down the details of a day's work; posterity will be as glad of the catalogue as we should be if we had such a record of how the door keeper at the Globe, and the man who kept the Park gates passed Saturday March 18th in the year of our Lord 1568.

And as such portraits as we have are almost invariably of the male sex, who strut more prominently across the stage, it seems worth while to take as model one of those many women who cluster in the shade. For a study of history and biography convinces any right minded person that these obscure figures occupy a place not unlike that of the showman's hand in the dance of the marionettes; and the finger is laid upon the heart. It is true that our simple eyes believed for many ages that the figures danced of their own accord, and cut what steps they chose; and the partial light which novelists and historians have begun to cast upon that dark and crowded place behind the scenes has done little as yet but show us how many wires there are, held in obscure hands, upon whose jerk or twist the whole figure of the dance depends. This preface leads us then to the point at which we began; we intend to look as steadily as we can at a little group, which lives at this moment (the 20th June, 1906); and seems for some reasons which we will give, to epitomise the qualities of many. It is a common case, because after all there are many young women, born of well-to-do, respectable, official parents; and they must all meet much the same problems, and there can be, unfortunately, but little variety in the answers they make.

There are five of them, all daughters they will ruefully explain to you: regretting this initial mistake it seems all through their lives on their parents' behalf. Further, they are divided into camps: two sisters oppose themselves to two sisters; the fifth vacillates equally between them. Nature has decreed that two shall inherit a stalwart pugnacious frame of mind, which applies itself to political economy and social problems successfully and not unhappily; while the other two she has made frivolous, domestic, of lighter and more sensitive temperaments. These two then are condemned to be what in the slang of the century is called 'the daughters at home'. Their sisters deciding to cultivate their brains, go to College, do well there, and marry Professors. Their careers have so much likeness to those of men themselves that it is scarcely worth while to make them the subject of special enquiry. The fifth sister is less marked in character than any of the others; but she marries when she is twenty-two so that she scarcely has time to develop the individual features of young ladydom which we set out to describe. In the two 'daughters at home' Phyllis and Rosamond, we will call them, we find excellent material for our enquiry.

A few facts will help us to set them in their places, before we begin to investigate. Phyllis is twenty-eight, Rosamond is twenty-four. In person they are pretty, pink cheeked, vivacious; a curious eye will not find any regular beauty of feature; but their dress and demeanour give them the effect of beauty without its substance. They seem indigenous to the drawing-room, as though, born in silk evening robes, they had never trod a rougher earth than the Turkey carpet, or reclined on harsher ground than the arm chair or the sofa. To see them in a drawing-room full of well dressed men and women, is to see the merchant in the Stock Exchange, or the barrister in the Temple. This, every motion and word proclaims, is their native air; their place of business, their professional arena. Here, clearly, they practise the arts in which they have been instructed since childhood. Here, perhaps, they win their victories and earn their bread. But it would be as unjust as it would be easy to press this metaphor till it suggested that the comparison was appropriate and complete in all its parts. It fails; but where it fails and why it fails it will take some time and attention to discover.

You must be in a position to follow these young ladies home, and to hear their comments over the bedroom candle. You must be by them when they wake next morning; and you must attend their progress throughout the day. When you have done this, not for one day but for many days then you will be able to calculate the values of those impressions which are to be received by night in the drawing-room.

This much may be retained of the metaphor already used; that the drawing-room scene represents work to them and not play. So much is made quite clear by the scene in the carriage going home. Lady Hibbert is a severe critic of such perform-ances; she has noted whether her daughters looked well, spoke well, behaved well; whether they attracted the right people and repelled the wrong; whether on the whole the impression they left was favourable. From the multiplicity and minuteness of her comments it is easy to see that two hours' entertainment is, for artists of this kind, a very delicate and complicated piece of work. Much it seems, depends upon the way they acquit themselves. The daughters answer submissively and then keep silence, whether their mother praises or blames: and her censure is severe. When they are alone at last, and they share a modest sized bedroom at the top of a great ugly house; they stretch their arms and begin to sigh with relief. Their talk is not very edifying; it is the 'shop' of business men; they calculate their profits and their losses and have clearly no interest at heart except their own. And yet you may have heard them chatter of books and plays and pictures as though these were the things they most cared about; to discuss them was the only motive of a 'party'.

Yet you will observe also in this hour of unlovely candour something which is also very sincere, but by no means ugly. The sisters were frankly fond of each other. Their affection has taken the form for the most part of a free masonship which is anything but sentimental; all their hopes and fears are in common; but it is a genuine feeling, profound in spite of its prosaic exterior. They are strictly honourable in all their dealings together; and there is even something chivalrous in the attitude of the younger sister to the elder. She, as the weaker by reason of her greater age, must always have the best of things. There is some pathos also in the gratitude with which Phyllis accepts the advantage. But it grows late, and in respect for their complexions, these business-like young women remind each other that it is time to put out the light.

In spite of this forethought they are fain to sleep on after they are called in the morning. But Rosamond jumps up, and shakes Phyllis.

'Phyllis we shall be late for breakfast.'

There must have been some force in this argument, for Phyllis got out of bed and began silently to dress. But their haste allowed them to put on their clothes with great care and dexterity, and the result was scrupulously surveyed by each sister in turn before they went down. The clock struck nine as they came into the breakfast room: their father was already there, kissed each daughter perfunctorily, passed his cup for coffee, read his paper and disappeared. It was a silent meal. Lady Hibbert breakfasted in her room; but after breakfast they had to visit her, to receive her orders for the day, and while one wrote notes for her the other went to arrange lunch and dinner with the cook. By eleven they were free, for the time, and met in the schoolroom where Doris the youngest sister, aged sixteen, was writing an essay upon the Magna Charter in French. Her complaints at the interruption – for she was dreaming of a first class already – met with no honour. 'We must sit here, because there's nowhere else to sit,' remarked Rosamond. 'You needn't think we want your company,' added Phyllis. But these remarks were spoken without bitterness, as the mere commonplaces of daily life.

In deference to their sister, however, Phyllis took up a volume of Anatole France, and Rosamond opened the 'Greek Studies' of Walter Pater.[1] They read for some minutes in silence; then a maid knocked, breathless, with a message that 'Her Ladyship wanted the young ladies in the drawing-room.' They groaned; Rosamond offered to go alone; Phyllis said no, they were both victims; and wondering what the errand was they went sulkily downstairs. Lady Hibbert was impatiently waiting them.

'O there you are at last,' she exclaimed. 'Your father has sent round to say he's asked Mr Middleton and Sir Thomas Carew to lunch. Isn't that troublesome of him! I can't think what drove him to ask them, and there's no lunch – and I see you haven't arranged the flowers, Phyllis; and Rosamond I want you to put a clean tucker in my maroon gown. O dear, how thoughtless men are.'

The daughters were used to these insinuations against their father: on the whole they took his side, but they never said so.

They silently departed now on their separate errands: Phyllis had to go out and buy flowers and an extra dish for lunch; and Rosamond sat down to her sewing.

Their tasks were hardly done in time for them to change for lunch; but at 1.30 they came pink and smiling into the pompous great drawing-room. Mr Middleton was Sir William Hibbert's secretary; a young man of some position and prospects, as Lady Hibbert defined him; who might be encouraged. Sir Thomas was an official in the same office, solid and gouty, a handsome piece on the board, but of no individual importance.

At lunch then there was some sprightly conversation between Mr Middleton and Phyllis, while their elders talked platitudes, in sonorous deep voices. Rosamond sat rather silent, as was her wont; speculating keenly upon the character of the secretary, who might be her brother-in-law; and checking certain theories she had made by every fresh word he spoke. By open consent, Mr Middleton was her sister's game; she did not trespass. If one could have read her thoughts, while she listened to Sir Thomas's stories of India in the Sixties, one would have found that she was busied in somewhat abstruse calculations; Little Middleton, as she called him, was not half a bad sort; he had brains; he was, she knew, a good son, and he would make a good husband. He was well to do also, and would make his way in the service. On the other hand her psychological acuteness told her that he was narrow minded, without a trace of imagination or intellect, in the sense she understood it; and she knew enough of her sister to know that she would never love this efficient active little man, although she would respect him. The question was should she marry him? This was the point she had reached when Lord Mayo was assassinated;[2] and while her lips murmured ohs and ahs of horror, her eyes were telegraphing across the table, 'I am doubtful.' If she had nodded her sister would have begun to practise those arts by which many proposals had been secured already. Rosamond, however, did not yet know enough to make up her mind. She telegraphed merely 'Keep him in play.'

The gentlemen left soon after lunch, and Lady Hibbert prepared to go and lie down. But before she went she called Phyllis to her.

'Well my dear,' she said, with more affection than she had shown yet, 'did you have a pleasant lunch? Was Mr Middleton agreeable?' She patted her daughter's cheek, and looked keenly into her eyes.

Some petulancy came across Phyllis, and she answered listlessly. 'O he's not a bad little man; but he doesn't excite me.'

Lady Hibbert's face changed at once: if she had seemed a benevolent cat playing with a mouse from philanthropic motives before, she was the real animal now in sober earnest.

'Remember,' she snapped, 'this can't go on for ever. Try and be a little less selfish, my dear.' If she had sworn openly, her words could not have been less pleasant to hear.

She swept off, and the two girls looked at each other, with expressive contortions of the lips.

'I couldn't help it,' said Phyllis, laughing weakly. 'Now let's have a respite. Her Ladyship won't want us till four.'

They mounted to the schoolroom, which was now empty; and threw themselves into deep arm chairs. Phyllis lit a cigarette, and Rosamond sucked peppermints, as though they induced to thought.

'Well, my dear,' said Phyllis at last, 'what do we decide? It is June now; our parents give me till July: little Middleton is the only one.'

'Except –' began Rosamond.

'Yes, but it is no good thinking of him.'

'Poor old Phyllis! Well, he's not a bad man.'

'Clean sober, truthful industrious. O we should make a model pair! You should stay with us in Derbyshire.'

'You might do better,' went on Rosamond; with the considering air of a judge. 'On the other hand, they won't stand much more.' 'They' intimated Sir William and Lady Hibbert.

'Father asked me yesterday what I could do if I didn't marry. I had nothing to say.'

'No, we were educated for marriage.'

'*You* might have done something better. Of course I'm a fool so it doesn't matter.'

'And I think marriage the best thing there is – if one were allowed to marry the man one wants.'

'O I know: it is beastly. Still there's no escaping facts.'

'Middleton,' said Rosamond briefly. 'He's the fact at present. Do you care for him?'

'Not in the least.'

'Could you marry him?'

'If her Ladyship made me.'

'It might be a way out, at any rate.'

'What d'you make of him now?' asked Phyllis, who would have accepted or rejected any man on the strength of her sister's advice. Rosamond, possessed of shrewd and capable brains, had been driven to feed them exclusively upon the human character and as her science was but little obscured by personal prejudice, her results were generally trustworthy.

'He's very good,' she began; 'moral qualities excellent: brains fair: he'll do well of course: not a scrap of imagination or romance: he'd be very just to you.'

'In short we would be a worthy pair: something like our parents!'

'The question is,' went on Rosamond; 'is it worth while going through another year of slavery, till the next one comes along? And who is the next? Simpson, Rogers, Leiscetter.'

At each name her sister made a face.

'The conclusion seems to be: mark time and keep up appearances.'

'O let's enjoy ourselves while we may! If it weren't for you, Rosamond, I should have married a dozen times already.'

'You'd have been in the divorce court my dear.'

'I'm too respectable for that, really. I'm very weak without you. And now let's talk of your affairs.'

'My affairs can wait,' said Rosamond resolutely. And the two young women discussed their friends' characters, with some acuteness and not a little charity till it was time to change once more. But two features of their talk are worth remark. First, that they held intellect in great reverence and made that a cardinal point in their enquiry; secondly that whenever they suspected an unhappy home life, or a disappointed attachment, even in the case of the least attractive, their judgments were invariably gentle and sympathetic.

At four they drove out with Lady Hibbert to pay calls. This performance consisted in driving solemnly to one house after another where they had dined or hoped to dine, and depositing two or three cards in the servant's hand. At one place they entered and drank a cup of tea, and talked of the weather for precisely fifteen minutes. They wound up with a slow passage through the Park, making one of the procession of gay carriages which travel at a foot's pace at that hour round the statue of Achilles. Lady Hibbert wore a permanent and immutable smile.

By six o'clock they were home again and found Sir William entertaining an elderly cousin and his wife at tea. These people could be treated without ceremony, and Lady Hibbert went off to lie down; and left her daughters to ask how John was, and whether Milly had got over the measles. 'Remember; we dine out at eight, William,' she said, as she left the room.

Phyllis went with them; the party was given by a distinguished judge, and she had to entertain a respectable K.C.; her efforts in one direction at least might be relaxed; and her mother's eye regarded her with indifference. It was like a draught of clear cold water, Phyllis reflected, to talk with an intelligent elderly man upon impersonal subjects. They did not theorise, but he told her facts and she was glad to realise that the world was full of solid things, which were independent of her life.

When they left she told her mother that she was going on to the Tristrams, to meet Rosamond there. Lady Hibbert pursed up her mouth, shrugged her shoulders and said 'very well,' as though she would have objected if she could have laid her hands on a sufficiently good reason. But Sir William was waiting, and a frown was the only argument.

So Phyllis went separately to the distant and unfashionable quarter of London where the Tristrams lived. That was one of the many enviable parts of their lot. The stucco fronts, the irreproachable rows of Belgravia and South Kensington seemed to Phyllis the type of her lot; of a life trained to grow in an ugly pattern to match the staid ugliness of its fellows. But if one lived here in Bloomsbury, she began to theorise waving with her hand as her cab passed through the great tranquil squares, beneath the pale green of umbrageous trees, one might grow up as one liked. There was room, and freedom, and in the roar and splendour of the Strand she read the live realities of the world from which her stucco and her pillars protected her so completely.

Her cab stopped before some lighted windows which, open in the summer night, let some of the talk and life within spill out upon the pavement. She was impatient for the door to open which was to let her enter, and partake. When she stood, however, within the room, she became conscious of her own appearance which, as she knew by heart, was on these occasions, like that of ladies whom Romney painted.[3] She saw herself enter into the smokey room where people sat on the floor, and the host wore a shooting jacket, with her arch little head held high, and her mouth pursed as though for an epigram. Her white silk and her cherry ribbons made her conspicuous. It was with some feeling of the difference between her and the rest that she sat very silent scarcely taking advantage of the openings that were made for her in the talk. She kept looking round at the dozen people who were sitting there, with a sense of bewilderment. The talk was of certain pictures then being shown, and their merits were discussed from a somewhat technical standpoint. Where was Phyllis to begin? She had seen them; but she knew that her platitudes would never stand the test of question and criticism to which they would be exposed. Nor, she knew, was there any scope here for those feminine graces which could veil so much. The time was passed; for the discussion was hot and serious, and no one of the combatants wished to be tripped by illogical devices. So she sat and watched, feeling like a bird with wings pinioned; and more acutely, because more genuinely, uncomfortable than she had ever been at ball or play. She repeated to herself the little bitter axiom that she had fallen between two stools; and tried meanwhile to use her brains soberly upon what was being said. Rosamond hinted from across the room that she was in the same predicament.

At last the disputants dissolved, and talk became general once more; but no one apologised for the concentrated character it had borne, and general conversation, the Miss Hibberts found, if it did occupy itself with more trivial subjects, tended to be scornful of the commonplace, and knew no hesitation in saying so. But it was amusing; and Rosamond acquitted herself creditably in discussing a certain character which came into question; although she was surprised to find that her most profound discoveries were taken as the starting point of further investigations, and represented no conclusions.

Moreover, the Miss Hibberts were surprised and a little dismayed to discover how much of their education had stuck to them. Phyllis could have beaten herself the next moment for her instinctive disapproval of some jest against Christianity which the Tristrams uttered and applauded as lightly as though religion was a small matter.

Even more amazing to the Miss Hibberts however was the manner in which their own department of business was transacted; for they supposed that even in this odd atmosphere 'the facts of life' were important. Miss Tristram, a young woman of great beauty, and an artist of real promise, was discussing marriage with a gentleman who might easily as far as one could judge, have a personal interest in the question. But the freedom and frankness with which they both explained their views and theorised upon the whole question of love and matrimony, seemed to put the whole thing in a new and sufficiently startling light. It fascinated the young ladies more than anything they had yet seen or heard. They had flattered themselves that every side and view of the subject was known to them; but this was something not only new, but unquestionably genuine.

'I have never yet had a proposal; I wonder what it feels like,' said the candid considering voice of the younger Miss Tristram; and Phyllis and Rosamond felt that they ought to produce their experiences for the instruction of the company. But then they could not adopt this strange new point of view, and their experiences after all were of a different quality entirely. Love to them was something induced by certain calculated actions; and it was cherished in ball rooms, in scented conservatories, by glances of the eyes, flashes of the fan, and faltering suggestive accents. Love here was a robust, ingenuous thing which stood out in the daylight, naked and solid, to be tapped and scrutinised as you thought best. Even were they free to love as they chose, Phyllis and Rosamond felt very doubtful that they could love in this way. With the rapid impulse of youth they condemned themselves utterly, and determined that all efforts at freedom were in vain: long captivity had corrupted them both within and without.

They sat thus, unconscious of their own silence, like people shut out from some merrymaking in the cold and the wind; invisible to the feasters within. But in reality the presence of these two silent and hungry eyed young women was felt to be oppressive by all the people there; although they did not exactly know why; perhaps they were bored. The Miss Tristrams, however, felt themselves responsible; and Miss Sylvia Tristram, the younger, as the result of a whisper, undertook a private conversation with Phyllis. Phyllis snatched at it like a dog at a bone;

indeed her face wore a gaunt ravenous expression, as she saw the moments fly, and the substance of this strange evening remained beyond her grasp. At least, if she could not share, she might explain what forbade her. She was longing to prove to herself that there were good reasons for her impotence; and if she felt that Miss Sylvia was a solid woman in spite of her impersonal generalisations, there was hope that they might meet some day on common ground. Phyllis had an odd feeling, when she leant forward to speak, of searching feverishly through a mass of artificial frivolities to lay hands on the solid grain of pure self which, she supposed lay hid somewhere.

'O Miss Tristram,' she began, 'you are all so brilliant. I do feel frightened.'

'Are you laughing at us,' asked Sylvia.

'Why should I laugh? Don't you see what a fool I feel?'

Sylvia began to see, and the sight interested her.

'Yours is such a wonderful life; it is so strange to us.'

Sylvia who wrote and had a literary delight in seeing herself reflected in strange looking-glasses, and of holding up her own mirror to the lives of others, settled herself to the task with gusto. She had never considered the Hibberts as human beings before; but had called them 'young ladies'. She was all the more ready now therefore to revise her mistake; both from vanity and from real curiosity.

'What do you do?' she demanded suddenly, in order to get to business at once.

'What do I do?' echoed Phyllis. 'O order dinner and arrange the flowers!'

'Yes, but what's your trade,' pursued Sylvia, who was determined not to be put off with phrases.

'*That's* my trade; I wish it wasn't! Really Miss Tristram, you must remember that most young ladies are slaves; and you mustn't insult me because you happen to be free.'

'O do tell me,' broke forth Sylvia, 'exactly what you mean. I want to know. I like to know about people. After all you know, the human soul is the thing.'

'Yes,' said Phyllis, anxious to keep from theories. 'But our life's so simple and so ordinary. You must know dozens like us.'

'I know your evening dresses,' said Sylvia; 'I see you pass before me in beautiful processions, but I have never yet heard you speak. Are you solid all through?' It struck her that this tone jarred upon Phyllis: so she changed.

'I daresay we are sisters. But why are we so different outside?'

'O no, we're not sisters,' said Phyllis bitterly; 'at least I pity you if we are. You see, we are brought up just to come out in the evening and make pretty speeches, and well, marry I suppose, and of course we might have gone to college if we'd wanted to; but as we didn't we're just accomplished.'

'We never went to college,' said Sylvia.

'And you're not accomplished? Of course you and your sister are the real thing, and Rosamond and I are frauds: at least I am. But don't you see it all now and don't you see what an ideal life yours is?'

'I can't see why you shouldn't do what you like, as we do,' said Sylvia, looking round the room.

'Do you think we could have people like this? Why, we can never ask a friend, except when our parents are away.'

'Why not?'

'We haven't a room, for one thing: and then we should never be allowed to do it. We are daughters, until we become married women.'

Sylvia considered her a little grimly. Phyllis understood that she had spoken with the wrong kind of frankness about love.

'Do you want to marry?' asked Sylvia.

'Can you ask? You are an innocent young thing – but of course you're quite right. It should be for love, and all the rest of it. But,' continued Phyllis, desperately speaking the truth, 'we can't think of it in that way. We want so many things, that we can never see marriage alone as it really is or ought to be. It is always mixed up with so much else. It means freedom and friends and a house of our own, and oh all the things you have already! Does that seem to you very dreadful and very mercenary?'

'It does seem rather dreadful; but not mercenary I think. I should write if I were you.'

'O there you go again, Miss Tristram!' exclaimed Phyllis in comic despair. 'I cannot make you understand that for one thing we haven't the brains; and for another, if we had them we couldn't use them. Mercifully the Good Lord made us fitted for our station. Rosamond might have done something; she's too old now.'

'My God,' exclaimed Sylvia. 'What a Black Hole! I should burn, shoot, jump out of the window; at least do something!'

'What?' asked Phyllis sardonically. 'If you were in our place you might; but I don't think you could be. O no,' she went on in a lighter and more cynical tone, 'this is our life, and we have to make the best of it. Only I want you to understand why it is that we come here and sit silent. You see, this is the life we should like to lead; and now I rather doubt that we can. You,' she indicated all the room, 'think us merely fashionable minxes; so we are, almost. But we might have been something better. Isn't it pathetic?' She laughed her dry little laugh.

'But promise me one thing, Miss Tristram: that you will come and see us, and that you will let us come here sometimes. Now Rosamond, we must really go.'

They left, and in the cab Phyllis wondered a little at her outburst; but felt that she had enjoyed it. They were both somewhat excited; and anxious to analyse their discomfort, and find out what it meant. Last night they had driven home at this hour in a more sullen but at the same time in a more self-satisfied temper; they were bored by what they had done, but they knew they had done it well. And they had the satisfaction of feeling that they were fit for far better things. Tonight they were not bored; but they did not feel that they had acquitted themselves well when they had the chance. The bedroom conference was a little dejected; in penetrating to her real self Phyllis had let in some chill gust of air to that closely guarded place; what did she really want, she asked herself? What was she fit for? to criticise both worlds and feel that neither gave her what she needed. She was too genuinely depressed to state the case to her sister; and her fit of honesty left her with the conviction that talking did no good; and if she could do anything, it must be done by herself. Her last thoughts that night were that it was rather a relief that Lady Hibbert had arranged a full day for them tomorrow: at any rate she need not think; and river parties were amusing.

The Mysterious Case
of Miss V.

It is a commonplace that there is no loneliness like that of one who finds himself alone in a crowd; novelists repeat it; the pathos is undeniable; and now, since the case of Miss V., I at least have come to believe it. Such a story as hers and her sister's – but it is characteristic that in writing of them one name seems instinctively to do for both – indeed one might mention a dozen such sisters in one breath. Such a story is scarcely possible except in London. In the country there would have been the butcher or the postman or the parson's wife; but in a highly civilised town the civilities of human life are narrowed to the least possible space. The butcher drops his meat down the area; the postman shoves his letter into the box, and the parson's wife has been known to hurl the pastoral missives through the same convenient breach: no time, they all repeat, must be wasted. So, though the meat remain uneaten, the letters unread, and the pastoral comments disobeyed, no one is any the wiser; until there comes a day when these functionaries tacitly conclude that no. 16 or 23 need be attended to no longer. They skip it, on their rounds, and poor Miss J. or Miss V. drops out of the closeknit chain of human life; and is skipped by everyone and for ever.

The ease with which such a fate befalls you suggests that it is really necessary to assert yourself in order to prevent yourself from being skipped; how could you ever come to life again if the butcher, the postman and the policeman made up their minds to ignore you? It is a terrible fate; I think I will knock over a chair at this moment; now the lodger beneath knows that I am alive at any rate.

But to return to the mysterious case of Miss V., in which initial, be it understood is concealed the person also of Miss Janet V.: it is hardly necessary to split one letter into two parts.

They have been gliding about London for some fifteen years; you were to find them in certain drawing-rooms or picture galleries, and when you said, 'Oh how d'you do Miss V.' as though you have been in the habit of meeting her every day of your life, she would answer, 'Isn't it a pleasant day,' or 'What bad weather we are having' and then you moved on and she seemed to melt into some armchair or chest of drawers. At any rate you thought no more of her until she detached herself from the furniture in a year's time perhaps, and the same things were said over again.

A tie of blood – or whatever the fluid was that ran in Miss V.'s veins – made it my particular fate to run against her – or pass through her or dissipate her, whatever the phrase may be – more constantly perhaps than any other person, until this little performance became almost a habit. No party or concert or gallery seemed quite complete unless the familiar grey shadow was part of it; and when, some time ago, she ceased to haunt my path, I knew vaguely that something was missing. I will not exaggerate and say that I knew that she was missing; but there is no insincerity in using the neuter term.

Thus in a crowded room I began to find myself gazing round in nameless dissatisfaction; no, everyone seemed to be there – but surely there was something lacking in furniture or curtains – or was it that a print was moved from the wall?

Then one morning early, wakening at dawn indeed, I cried aloud, Mary V. Mary V!! It was the first time, I am sure that anyone had ever cried her name with such conviction; generally it seemed a colourless epithet, used merely to round a period. But my voice did not as I half expected, summon the person or semblance of Miss V. before me: the room remained vague. All day long my own cry echoed in my brain; till I made certain that at some street corner or another I should come across her as usual, and see her fade away, and be satisfied. Still, she came not; and I think I was discontented. At any rate the strange fantastic plan came into my head as I lay awake at night, a mere whim at first, which grew serious and exciting by degrees, that I would go and call on Mary V. in person.

O how mad and odd and amusing it seemed, now that I thought of it! – to track down the shadow, to see where she lived and if she lived, and talk to her as though she were a person like the rest of us!

Consider how it would seem to set out in an omnibus to visit the shadow of a blue bell in Kew Gardens, when the sun stands halfway down the sky! or to catch the down from a dandelion! at midnight in a Surrey meadow. Yet it was a much more fantastic expedition than any of these that I proposed; and as I put on my clothes to start I laughed and laughed to think that such substantial preparation was needed for my task. Boots and hat for Mary V.! It seemed incredibly incongruous.

At length I reached the flat where she lived, and on looking at the signboard I found it stated ambiguously – like the rest of us – that she was both out and in. At her door, high up in the topmost storey of the building, I knocked and rang, and waited and scrutinised; no one came; and I began to wonder if shadows could die, and how one buried them; when the door was gently opened by a maid. Mary V. had been ill for two months; she had died yesterday morning, at the very hour when I called her name. So I shall never meet her shadow any more.

The Journal of
Mistress Joan Martyn

My readers may not know, perhaps, who I am. Therefore, although such a practice is unusual and unnatural – for we know how modest writers are – I will not hesitate to explain that I am Miss Rosamond Merridew, aged forty-five – my frankness is consistent! – and that I have won considerable fame among my profession for the researches I have made into the system of land tenure in mediaeval England. Berlin has heard my name; Frankfurt would give a soiree in my honour; and I am not absolutely unknown in one or two secluded rooms in Oxford and in Cambridge. Perhaps I shall put my case more cogently, human nature being what it is, if I state that I have exchanged a husband and a family and a house in which I may grow old for certain fragments of yellow parchment; which only a few people can read and still fewer would care to read if they could. But as a mother, so I read sometimes not without curiosity in the literature of my sex, cherishes most the ugliest and stupidest of her offspring, so a kind of maternal passion has sprung up in my breast for these shrivelled and colourless little gnomes; in real life I see them as cripples with fretful faces, but all the same, with the fire of genius in their eyes. I will not expound that sentence; it would be no more likely to succeed than if that same mother to whom I compare myself took pains to explain that her cripple was really a beautiful boy, more fair than all his brothers.

At any rate, my investigations have made a travelling pedlar of me; save that it is my habit to buy and not to sell. I present myself at old farm houses, decayed halls, parsonages, church vestries always with the same demand. Have you any old papers to show me? As you may imagine the palmy days for this kind of sport are over; age has become the most merchantable of qualities; and the state moreover with its Commissions has put an end for the most part to the enterprise of individuals. Some official, I am often told, has promised to come down and inspect their documents; and the favour of the 'State' which such a promise carries with it, robs my poor private voice of all its persuasion.

Still it is not for me to complain, looking back as I can look back, upon some very fine prizes that will have been of real interest to the historian, and upon others that because they are so fitful and so minute in their illumination please me even better. A sudden light upon the legs of Dame Elizabeth Partridge sends its beams over the whole state of England, to the King upon his throne; she wanted stockings! and no other need impresses you in quite the same way with the reality of mediaeval legs; and therefore with the reality of mediaeval bodies, and so, proceeding upward step by step, with the reality of mediaeval brains; and there you stand at the centre of all ages: middle beginning or end. And this brings me to a further confession of my own virtues. My researches into the system of land tenure in the 13th, 14th and 15th Centuries have been made doubly valuable, I am assured, by the remarkable gift I have for presenting them in relation to the life of the time. I have borne in mind that the intricacies of the land tenure were not always the most important facts in the lives of men and women and children; I have often made so bold as to hint that the subtleties which delight us so keenly were more a proof of our ancestors' negligence than a proof of their astonishing painstaking. For what sane man, I have had the audacity to remark, could have spent his time in complicating his laws for the benefit of half a dozen antiquaries who were to be born five centuries after he was in the grave?

We will not here discuss this argument on whose behalf I have given and taken many shrewd blows; I introduce the question merely to explain why it is that I have made all these enquiries subsidiary to certain pictures of the family life which I have introduced into my text; as the flower of all these intricate roots; the flash of all this scraping of flint.

If you read my work called 'The Manor Rolls' you will be pleased or disgusted according to your temperament by certain digressions which you will find there.

I have not scrupled to devote several pages of large print to an attempt to show, vividly as in a picture, some scene from the life of the time; here I knock at the serf's door, and find him roasting rabbits he has poached; I show you the Lord of the Manor setting out on some journey, or calling his dogs to him for a walk in the fields, or sitting in the high backed chair inscribing laborious figures upon a glossy sheet of parchment. In another room I show you Dame Elinor, at work with her needle; and by her on a lower stool sits her daughter stitching too, but less assiduously. 'Child, thy husband will be here before thy house linen is ready,' reproves the mother.

Ah, but to read this at large you must study my book! The critics have always threatened me with two rods; first, they say, such digressions are all very well in a history of the time, but they have nothing to do with the system of mediaeval land tenure; secondly, they complain that I have no materials at my side to stiffen these words into any semblance of the truth. It is well known that the period I have chosen is more bare than any other of private records; unless you choose to draw all your inspiration from the *Paston Letters* you must be content to imagine merely, like any other story teller. And that, I am told, is a useful art in its place; but it should be allowed to claim no relationship with the sterner art of the Historian. But here, again, I verge upon that famous argument which I carried on once with so much zeal in the *Historian's Quarterly*. We must make way with our introduction, or some wilful reader may throw down the book and profess to have mastered its contents already: O the old story! Antiquaries' Quarrels! Let me draw a line here then so——and put the whole of this question of right and wrong, truth and fiction behind me.

On a June morning two years ago, it chanced that I was driving along the Thetford road from Norwich to East Harling. I had been on some expedition, a wild goose chase it was, to recover some documents which I believed to lie buried in the ruins of Caister Abbey. If we were to spend a tithe of the sums that we spend yearly upon excavating Greek cities in excavating our own ruins what a different tale the Historian would have to tell!

Such was the theme of my meditations; but nevertheless one eye, my archaeological eye, kept itself awake to the landscape through which we passed. And it was in obedience to a telegram from this that I leapt up in the carriage, at a certain point and directed the driver to turn sharply to the left. We passed down a regular avenue of ancient elm trees; but the bait which drew me was a little square picture, framed delicately between green boughs at the far end, in which an ancient doorway was drawn distinctly in lines of carved white stone.

As we approached, the doorway proved to be encircled by long low walls of buff coloured plaster; and on top of them, at no great distance was the roof of ruddy tiles, and finally I beheld in front of me the whole of the dignified little house, built like the letter E with the middle notch smoothed out of it.

Here was one of those humble little old Halls, then, which survive almost untouched, and practically unknown for centuries and centuries, because they are too insignificant to be pulled down or rebuilt; and their owners are too poor to be ambitious. And the descendants of the builder go on living here, with that curious unconsciousness that the house is in any way remarkable which serves to make them as much a part of it, as the tall chimney which has grown black with generations of kitchen smoke. Of course a larger house might be preferable, and I doubt not that they would hesitate to sell this old one, if a good offer were to be made for it. But that is the natural, and unself-conscious spirit which proves somehow how genuine the whole thing is. You can not be sentimental about a house you have lived in for five hundred years. This is the kind of place, I thought, as I stood with my hand on the bell, where the owners are likely to possess exquisite manuscripts, and sell them as easily to the first rag man who comes along, as they would sell their pig wash, or the timber from the park. My point of view is that of a morbid eccentric, after all, and these are the people of truly healthy nature. Can't they write? they will tell me; and what is the worth of old letters? I always burn mine – or use them to tie over jampots.

A maid came, at last, staring meditatively at me, as though she ought to have remembered my face and my business. 'Who lives here?' I asked her. 'Mr Martyn,' she gaped, as if I had asked the name of the reigning King of England. 'Is there a Mrs Martyn, and is she at home, and might I see her?' The girl waved to me to follow, and led me in silence to a person who could, presumably, undertake the responsibility of answering my strange questions.

I was shown across a large hall, panelled with oak, to a smaller room in which a rosy woman of my own age was using a machine upon a pair of trousers. She looked like a house-keeper; but she was, the maid whispered, Mrs Martyn.

She rose with a gesture that indicated that she was not precisely a lady to receive morning calls, but was nevertheless the person of authority, the mistress of the house; who had a right to know my business in coming there.

There are certain rules in the game of the antiquary, of which the first and simplest is that you must not state your object at the first encounter. 'I was passing by your door; and I took the liberty – I must tell you I am a great lover of the picturesque, to call, on the chance that I might be allowed to look over the house. It seems to me a particularly fine specimen.'

'Do you want to rent it, may I ask,' said Mrs Martyn, who spoke with a pleasant tinge of dialect.

'Do you let rooms then?' I questioned.

'O no,' rejoined Mrs Martyn, decisively: 'We never let rooms; I thought perhaps you wished to rent the whole house.'

'It's a little big for me; but still, I have friends.'

'As well, then,' broke in Mrs Martyn, cheerfully, setting aside the notion of profit, and looking merely to do a charitable act; 'I'm sure I should be very pleased to show you over the house – I don't know much about old things myself; and I never heard as the house was particular in any way. Still it's a pleasant kind of place – if you come from London.' She looked curiously at my dress and figure, which I confess felt more than usually bent beneath her fresh, and somewhat compassionate gaze; and I gave her the information she wanted. Indeed as we strolled through the long passages, pleasantly striped with bars of oak across the white wash, and looked into spotless little rooms with square green windows opening on the garden, and where I saw furniture that was spare but decent, we exchanged a considerable number of questions and answers. Her husband was a farmer on rather a large scale; but land had sunk terribly in value; and they were forced to live in the Hall now, which would not let; although it was far too large for them, and the rats were a nuisance. The Hall had been in her husband's family for many a year, she remarked with some slight pride; she did not know how long, but people said the Martyns had once been great people in the neighbourhood. She drew my attention to the 'y' in their name. Still she spoke with the very chastened and clear sighted pride of one who knows by hard personal experience how little nobility of birth avails, against certain material drawbacks, the poverty of the land, for instance, the holes in the roof, and the rapacity of rats.

Now although the place was scrupulously clean, and well kept there was a certain bareness in all the rooms, a prominence of huge oak tables, and an absence of other decorations than bright pewter cups and china plates which looked ominous to my inquisitive gaze. It seemed as though a great deal must have been sold, of those small portable things that make a room look furnished. But my hostess' dignity forbade me to suggest that her house had ever been other than it was at present. And yet I could not help fancying a kind of wistfulness in the way she showed me into rooms that were almost empty, compared the present poverty to days of greater affluence, and had it on the tip of her tongue to tell me that 'Things had once been better.' She seemed half apologetic, too, as she led me through a succession of bedrooms, and one or two rooms that might have served for sitting rooms if people had had leisure to sit there, as though she wished to show me that she was quite aware of the discrepancy between such a house and her own sturdy figure. All this being as it was, I did not like to ask the question that interested me most – whether they had any books? and I was beginning to feel that I had kept the good woman from her sewing machine long enough, when she suddenly looked out of the window, hearing a whistle below, and shouted something about coming in to dinner. Then she turned to me with some shyness, but an expression of hospitality, and begged me to 'Sit down to dinner' with them. 'John, my husband, knows a sight more than I do of these old things of his, and I know he's glad enough to find some one to talk to. It's in his blood, I tell him,' she laughed, and I saw no good reason why I should not accept the invitation. Now John did not fall so easily beneath any recognized heading as his wife did. He was a man of middle age and middle size, dark of hair and complexion, with a pallor of skin that did not seem natural to a farmer; and a drooping moustache which he smoothed slowly with one well shaped hand as he spoke. His eye was hazel and bright, but I fancied a hint of suspicion when its glance rested upon me. He began to speak however, with even more of a Norfolk accent than his wife; and his voice, and dress asserted that he was, in truth if not altogether in appearance, a solid Norfolk farmer.

He nodded merely when I told him that his wife had had the kindness to show me his house. And then, looking at her with a twinkle in his eye he remarked, 'If she had her way the old place would be left to the rats. The house is too big, and there are too many ghosts. Eh Betty.' She merely smiled, as though her share of the argument had been done long ago.

I thought to please him by dwelling upon its beauties, and its age; but he seemed little interested by my praises, munched largely of cold beef, and added 'ayes' and 'noes' indifferently.

A picture, painted perhaps in the time of Charles the First, which hung above his head, had so much the look of him had his collar and tweed been exchanged for a ruff and a silk doublet, that I made the obvious comparison.

'O aye,' he said, with no great show of interest, 'that's my grandfather; or my grandfather's grandfather. We deal in grandfathers here.'

'Was that the Martyn who fought at the Boyne,' asked Betty negligently while she pressed me to take another slice of beef.

'At the Boyne,' exclaimed her husband, with query and even irritation – 'Why, my good woman, you're thinking of Uncle Jasper. This fellow was in his grave long before the Boyne. His name's Willoughby,' he went on speaking to me, as though he wished me to understand the matter thoroughly; because a blunder about such a simple fact was unpardonable, even though the fact itself might not be of great interest.

'Willoughby Martyn: born 1625 died 1685: he fought at Marston Moor as Captain of a Troop of Norfolk men. We were always royalists. He was exiled in the Protectorate, went to Amsterdam; bought a bay horse off the Duke of Newcastle there; we have the breed still; he came back here at the Restoration, married Sally Hampton – of the Manor, but they died out last generation, and had six children, four sons and two daughters. He bought the Lower Meadow you know Betty,' he jerked at his wife, to goad her unaccountably sluggish memory.

'I call him to mind well enough now,' she answered, placidly.

'He lived here all the last part of his life; died of small pox, or what they called small pox then; and his daughter Joan caught it from him. They're buried in the same grave in the church yonder.' He pointed his thumb, and went on with his dinner. All this was volunteered as shortly and even curtly as though he were performing some necessary task, which from long famil-iarity had become quite uninteresting to him; though for some reason he had still to repeat it.

I could not help showing my interest in the story, although I was conscious that my questions did not entertain my host.

'You seem to have a queer liking for these old fathers of mine,' he commented, at last, with an odd little scowl of humorous irritation. 'You must show her the pictures after dinner, John,' put in his wife; 'and all the old things.'

'I should be immensely interested,' I said, 'but I must not take up your time.'

'O John knows a quantity about them; he's wonderful learned about pictures.'

'Any fool knows his own ancestors, Betty;' growled her husband; 'still, if you wish to see what we have, Madam, I shall be proud to show you.' The courtesy of the phrase, and the air with which he held the door open for me, made me remember the 'y' in his name.

He showed me round the Hall, pointing with a riding crop to one dark canvas after another; and rapping out two or three unhesitating words of description at each; they were hung apparently in chronological order, and it was clear in spite of the dirt and the dark that the late portraits were feebler examples of the art, and represented less distinguished looking heads. Military coats became less and less frequent and in the 18th century the male Martyns were represented in snuff coloured garments of a homely cut, and were briefly described a 'Farmers' or 'him who sold the Fen Farm' by their descendant. Their wives and daughters at length dropped out altogether, as though in time a portrait had come to be looked upon more as the necessary appendage of the head of the house, rather than as the right which beauty by itself could claim.

Still, I could trace no sign in the man's voice that he was following the decline of his family with his riding crop, for there was neither pride nor regret in his tone; indeed it kept its level note, as of one who tells a tale so well known that the words have been rubbed smooth of meaning.

'There's the last of them – my father,' he said at length, when he had slowly traversed the four sides of the Hall; I looked upon a crude canvas, painted in the early sixties I gathered, by some travelling painter with a literal brush. Perhaps the unskilful hand had brought out the roughness of the features and the harshness of the complexion; had found it easier to paint the farmer than to produce the subtle balance which, one might gather, blent in the father as in the son. The artist had stuffed his sitter into a black coat, and wound a stiff white tie round his neck; the poor gentleman had never felt at ease in them, yet.

'And now, Mr Martyn,' I felt bound to say, 'I can only thank you, and your wife for...'

'Stop a moment,' he interrupted, 'we're not done yet. There are the books.'

His voice had a half comic doggedness about it; like one who is determined, in spite of his own indifference to the undertaking, to make a thorough job of it.

He opened a door and bade me enter a small room, or rather office; for the table heaped with papers, and the walls lined with ledgers, suggested the room where business is transacted by the master of an estate. There were pads and brushes for ornament; and there were mostly dead animals, raising lifeless paws, and grinning, with plaster tongues, from various brackets and cases.

'These go back beyond the pictures;' he said, as he stooped and lifted a great parcel of yellow papers with an effort. They were not bound, or kept together in any way, save by a thick cord of green silk, with bars at either end; such as you use to transfix bundles of greasy documents – butcher's bills, and the year's receipts. 'That's the first lot,' he said ruffling the leaves with his fingers, like a pack of cards; 'that's no. 1: 1480 to 1500.' I gasped, as anyone may judge: but the temperate voice of Martyn reminded me that enthusiasm was out of place, here; indeed enthusiasm began to look like a very cheap article when contrasted with the genuine thing.

'Ah indeed; that's very interesting; may I look?' was all I said, though my undisciplined hand shook a little when the bundle was carelessly dropped into it. Mr Martyn indeed offered to fetch a duster before desecrating my white skin; but I assured him it was of no consequence, too eagerly perhaps, because I had feared that there might be some more substantial reason why I should not hold these precious papers.

While he bent down before a book case, I hastily looked at the first inscription on the parchment. 'The Journal of Mistress Joan Martyn,' I spelt out, 'kept by her at Martyn's Hall, in the county of Norfolk the year of our Lord 1480.'

'My grandmother Joan's diary,' interrupted Martyn, turning round with his arm full of books. 'Queer old lady she must have been. I could never keep a diary myself. Never kept one beyond the 10th of February, though I tried often. But here you see,' he leant over me, turning the pages, and pointing with his finger, 'here is January, February, March, April – so on – a whole twelve months.'

'Have you read it, then?' I asked, expecting, nay, hoping that he would say no.

'O yes, I've read it;' he remarked casually, as though that were but a simple undertaking. 'It took me some time to get used to the writing, and the old girl's spelling is odd. But there are some queer things in it. I learnt a deal about the land from her, one way and another.' He tapped it meditatively.

'Do you know her history too?' I asked.

'Joan Martyn,' he began in the voice of a showman, 'was born 1495. She was the daughter of Giles Martyn. She was his only daughter. He had three sons though; we always have sons. She wrote this diary when she was twenty-five. She lived here all her life – never married. Indeed she died at the age of thirty. I daresay you might see her tomb down there with the rest of them.'[4]

'Now this,' he said touching a thick book bound in parchment, 'is more interesting to my mind. This is the household book of Jasper for the year 1583. See how the old gentleman kept his accounts; what they eat and drank; how much meat and bread and wine cost; how many servants he kept – his horses, carriages, beds, furniture, everything. There's method for you. I have a set of ten of them.' He spoke of them with greater pride than I had heard him speak of any of his possessions yet.

'This one too makes good reading of a winter's night,' he went on. 'This is the Stud book of Willoughby; you remember Willoughby.'

'The one who bought the horse of the Duke, and died of small pox,' I repeated glibly.

'That's so,' he nodded. 'Now this is really fine stuff this one.' He went on, like a connoisseur, talking of some favourite brand of port. 'I wouldn't sell this for £20. Here are names, the pedigrees, the lives, values, descendants; all written out like a bible.' He rolled some of the strange old names of these dead horses upon his tongue, as though he relished the sound like wine. 'Ask my wife if I can't tell 'em all without the book,' he laughed, shutting it carefully and placing it on the shelf.

'These are the Estate books; they go down to this year; there's the last of 'em. Here's our family history.' He unrolled a long strip of parchment, upon which an elaborate genealogical tree had been inscribed, with many faded flourishes and extravagances of some mediaeval pen. The boughs spread so widely by degrees, that they were lopped unmercifully by the limits of the sheet – a husband depending for instance, with a family of ten children and no wife. Fresh ink at the base of all recorded the names of Jasper Martyn, my host, and his wife Elizabeth Clay: they had three sons. His finger travelled sagaciously down the tree, as though it were so well used to this occupation that it could almost be trusted to perform it by itself. Martyn's voice murmured on as though it repeated a list of Saints or Virtues in some monotonous prayer.

'Yes,' he concluded, rolling up the sheet and laying it by, 'I think I like those two best. I could say them through with my eyes shut. Horses or Grandfathers!'

'Do you study here a great deal then?' I asked, somewhat puzzled by this strange man.

'I've no time for study,' he returned, rather roughly, as tho' the farmer cropped up in him at my question. 'I like to read something easy in the winter nights; and in the morning too, if I wake early. I keep them by my bed sometimes. I say them to send myself to sleep. It's easy to know the names of one's own family. They come natural. But I was never any good at book learning, more's the pity.'

Asking my permission, he lit a pipe and began puffing forth great curls of smoke, as he ranged the volumes in order before him. But I kept No. One, the bundle of parchment sheets, in my hand, nor did he seem to miss it from the rest.

'You would be sorry to part with any of these, I daresay?' I hazarded, at last, covering my real eagerness with an attempt at a laugh.

'Part with them?' he returned, 'what should I part with them for?' The idea was evidently so remote that my question had not, as I feared, irritated his suspicions.

'No, no,' he went on, 'I find them far too useful for that. Why, Madam, these old papers have stood out for my rights in a court of law before now; besides, a man likes to keep his family round him; I should feel – well kind of lonely if you take my meaning, without my Grandfathers and Grandmothers, and Uncles and Aunts.' He spoke as though he confessed a weakness.

'O,' I said, 'I quite understand –'

'I daresay you have the same feeling yourself Madam and down here, in a lonely place like this, company means more than you could well believe. I often think I shouldn't know how to pass the time, if it weren't for my relations.'

No words of mine, or attempts at a report of his words, can give the curious impression which he produced as he spoke, that all these 'relations' Grandfathers of the time of Elizabeth, nay Grandmothers of the time of Edward the Fourth, were just, so to speak, brooding round the corner; there was none of the pride of 'ancestry' in his voice but merely the personal affection of a son for his parents. All generations seemed bathed in his mind in the same clear and equable light: it was not precisely the light of the present day, but it certainly was not what we commonly call the light of the past. And it was not romantic, it was very sober, and very broad and the figures stood out in it, solid and capable, with a great resemblance, I suspect, to what they were in the flesh.

It really needed no stretch of the imagination to perceive that Jasper Martyn might come in from his farm and his fields, and sit down here alone to a comfortable gossip with his 'relations;' whenever he chose; and that their voices were very nearly as audible to him as those of the labourers in the field below, which came floating in, upon the level afternoon sunlight through the open window.

But my original intention of asking whether he would sell, almost made me blush when I remembered it now: so irrelevant and so impertinent. And also, strange though it may seem, I had lost for the time my proper antiquarian zeal; all my zest for old things, and the little distinguishing marks of age, left me, because they seemed the trivial and quite immaterial accidents of large substantial things. There was really no scope for antiquarian ingenuity in the case of Mr Martyn's ancestors, anymore than it needed an antiquary to expound the history of the man himself.

They are, he would have told me, all flesh and blood like I am; and the fact that they have been dead for four or five centuries makes no more difference to them, than the glass you place over a canvas changes the picture beneath it.

But on the other hand, if it seemed impertinent to buy, it seemed natural, if perhaps a little simpleminded, to borrow.

'Well, Mr Martyn,' I said at length, with less eagerness and less trepidation than I could have thought possible under the circumstances, 'I am thinking of staying for a week or so in this neighbourhood – at the Swan at Gartham indeed – I should be much obliged to you if you would lend me these papers to look through during my stay. This is my card. Mr Lathom, (the great landowner of the place) will tell you all about me.' Instinct told me that Mr Martyn was not the man to trust the benevolent impulses of his heart.

'O Madam, there's no need to bother about that,' he said, carelessly, as though my request were not of sufficient importance to need his scrutiny. 'If these old papers please you, I'm

sure you're welcome to 'em.' He seemed a little surprised, however, so that I added, 'I take a great interest in family histories,
even when they're not my own.'

'It's amusing eno', I daresay, if you have the time,' he assented
politely; but I think his opinion of my intelligence was lowered.

'Which would you like,' he asked, stretching his hand
towards the Household Books of Jasper; and the Stud book of
Willoughby.

'Well I think I'll begin with your grandmother Joan,' I said; 'I
like beginning at the beginning.'

'O very well,' he smiled; 'though I don't think you'll find
anything out of the way in her; she was very much the same as
the rest of us – as far as I can see, not remarkable –'

But all the same, I walked off with Grandmother Joan beneath my arm; Betty insisted upon wrapping her in brown paper,
to disguise the queer nature of the package, for I refused to let
them send it over as they wished, by the boy who took the letters
on his bicycle.

(1)

The state of the times, which my mother tells me, is less safe and
less happy than when she was a girl, makes it necessary for us to
keep much within our own lands. After dark indeed, and the
sun sets terribly soon in January, we have to be safe behind the
hall Gates; my mother goes out as soon as the dark makes her
embroidery too dim to see, with the great keys on her arm. 'Is
everybody within doors?' she cries, and swings the bells out
upon the road, in case any of our men may still be working in
the fields. Then she draws the Gates close, clamps them with the
lock, and the whole world is barred away from us. I am very
bold and impatient sometimes, when the moon rises, over a

land gleaming with frost; and I think I feel the pressure of all this free and beautiful place – all England and the sea, and the lands beyond – rolling like sea waves, against our iron gates, breaking, and withdrawing – and breaking again – all through the long black night. Once I leapt from my bed, and ran to my mother's room, crying, 'Let them in. Let them in! We are starving!' 'Are the soldiers there, child,' she cried: 'or is it your father's voice?' She ran to the window, and together we gazed out upon the silver fields, and all was peaceful. But I could not explain what it was that I heard; and she bade me sleep, and be thankful that there were stout gates between me and the world.

But on other nights, when the wind is wild and the moon is sunk beneath hurrying clouds, I am glad to draw close to the fire, and to think that all those bad men who prowl in the lanes, and lie hidden in the woods at this hour cannot break through our great Gates, try as they will. Last night was such a night; they come often in Winter when my father is away in London, my brothers are with the army, save my little brother Jeremy, and my mother has to manage the farm, and order the people, and see that all our rights are looked to. We may not burn the tapers after the church bell has struck 8 times, and so we sit round the logs, with the priest, John Sandys, and one or two of the servants who sleep with us in the Hall. Then my mother, who cannot be idle even by fire light, winds her wool for her knitting, sitting in the great chair which stands by the cheek of the hearth. When her wool gets tangled she strikes a great blow with the iron rod, and sends the flames and the sparks spurting in showers; she stoops her head into the tawny light, and you see what a noble woman she is; in spite of age – she is more than forty – and the hard lines which much thought and watching have cut in her brow. She wears a fine linen cap, close fitting to the shape of her head, and her eyes are deep and stern, and her cheek is coloured like a healthy winter apple. It is a great thing to be the daughter of such a woman, and to hope that one day the same power may be mine. She rules us all.

Sir John Sandys, the priest, is, for all his sacred office, the servant of my mother; and does her will simply and querulously, and is never so happy as when she asks him for advice, and takes her own. But she would scold me well if I ever whispered such a thing: for she is the faithful daughter of the Church, and reverences her Priest. Again there are William and Anne, the servants who sit with us, because they are so old that my mother wishes them to share our fire. But William is so ancient, so curved with planting and digging, so bruised and battered by the sun and the wind that one might as well ask the pollard willow in the fen to share one's fire, or join one's talk. Still, his memory goes back a great way, and if he could tell us, as he sometimes tries to begin, of the things he has seen in his day, it would be curious to hear. Old Anne was my mother's nurse; she was mine; and still she mends our clothes, and knows more about household things than any, save my mother. She will tell you, too, the history of each chair and table or piece of tapestry in the house; but most of all she likes to discuss with mother and Sir John the men whom it would be most suitable for me to marry.

As long as the light serves it is my duty to read aloud – because I am the only one who can read though my mother can write, and spell words beyond the fashion of her time, and my father has sent me a manuscript from London; called The Palace of Glass, by Mr John Lydgate. It is a poem, written about Helen and the Siege of Troy.

Last night I read of Helen, and her beauty and her suitors, and the fair town of Troy and they listened silently; for though we none of us know where those places are, we see very well what they must have been like; and we can weep for the sufferings of the soldiers, and picture to ourselves the stately woman herself, who must have been, I think, something like my mother. My mother beats with her foot and sees the whole processions pass I know, from the way her eyes gleam, and her head tosses. 'It must have been in Cornwall,' said Sir John, 'where King Arthur lived with his knights. I remember stories I could tell you of all their doings, but my memory is dim.'

'Ah but there are fine stories of the Northmen, too,' broke in Anne; whose mother was from those parts; 'but I have sung them often to my Mister, and to you too Miss Joan.'

'Read on Joan, while there is light,' commanded my mother. Indeed, of all I think she listened closest, and was most vexed when the Curfew tolled from the Church nearby. Yet she called herself an old fool for listening to stories, when the accounts had still to be made up for my father in London.

When the light is out and I can no longer see to read, they begin talking of the state of the country; and telling dreadful stories of the plots and the battles and the bloody deeds that are going on all round us. But for all I can see, we are not worse now than we have always been; and we in Norfolk today are much the same as we were in the days of Helen, wherever she may have lived. Was not Jane Moryson carried off on the eve of her wedding only last year?

But anyhow, the story of Helen is old; my mother says it happened long before her day; and these robbings and burnings are going on now. So the talk makes me, and Jeremy too, tremble and think that every rattle of the big door, is the battering ram of some wandering highwayman.

It is far worse tho', when the time for bed comes, and the fire sinks, and we have to feel our way up the great stairs, and along the passages, where the windows shine grey, and so into our cold bed rooms. The window in my room is broken, and stuffed with straw, but gusts come in and lift the tapestry on the wall, till I think that horses and men in armour are charging down upon me. My prayer last night was, that the great gates might hold fast, and all robbers and murderers might pass us by.

(2)

The dawn, even when it is cold and melancholy, never fails to shoot through my limbs as with arrows of sparkling piercing ice. I pull aside the thick curtains, and search for the first glow in the sky which shows that life is breaking through. And with my cheek leant upon the window pane I like to fancy that I am pressing as closely as can be upon the massy wall of time, which is for ever lifting and pulling and letting fresh spaces of life in upon us. May it be mine to taste the moment before it has spread itself over the rest of the world! Let me taste the newest and the freshest. From my window I look down upon the Church yard, where so many of my ancestors are buried, and in my prayer I pity those poor dead men who toss perpetually on the old recurring waters; for I see them, circling and eddying forever upon a pale tide. Let us, then, who have the gift of the present, use it and enjoy it: That I confess, is part of my morning prayer.

It rained steadily today, so that I had to spend the morning with my sewing. My mother was writing her letter to my father which John Ashe will take with him to London next week. My thoughts naturally dwelt upon this journey, and upon the great city which perhaps I may never see, though I am for ever dreaming of it. You start at dawn; for it is well to spend few nights on the road. John travels with three other men, bound to the same place; and I have often seen them set forth, and longed to ride with them. They gather in the courtyard, while the stars are still in the sky; and the people of the neighbourhood come out wrapped in cloaks and strange garments, and my mother carries out a tankard of strong Ale to each traveller; and gives it to him from her own hand. Their horses are laden with packs before and behind, but not so as to hinder them from starting out in a gallop if need be; and the men are well armed, and closely dressed in fur lined habits, for the winter days are short and cold, and maybe they will sleep beneath a hedge. It is a gallant sight in the dawn; for the horses champ and fret to be gone; the people cluster round. They wish their God speeds and their last messages to friends in London; and as the clock strikes four they wheel about, salute my mother and the rest, and turn sharply on their road. Many young men and women too, follow them some paces on the way till the mist comes between, for often men who set forth thus in the dawn, never ride home again.

I picture them riding all day along the white roads, and I see them dismount at the shrine of our Lady and do homage, pray to her for a safe journey. There is but one road, and it passes through vast lands, where no men live, but only those who have murdered or robbed; for they may not dwell with others in towns, but must pass their lives with the wild beasts, who murder also, and eat the clothes from your back. It is a fearful ride; but, truly, I think I should like to go that way once, and pass over the land, like a ship at sea.

At midday they reach an Inn – for there are Inns at all the stages upon the journey to London, where a traveller may rest in safety. The landlord will tell you the state of the road, and he will ask you of your adventures, so that he may give warning to others who travel the same way. But you must press on, to reach your sleeping place before the dark lets loose all those fierce creatures, who have lain hidden in the day. John has often told me how as the sun comes from the sky silence falls on the company, and each man has his gun swung beneath his hand, and even the horses prick their ears and need no urging. You reach the crest of the road, and look fearfully beneath you, lest something moves in the shade of the fir trees by the wayside. And then Robin, the cheerful Miller, shouts a snatch of a song, and they take heart, and step bravely down the hill, talking lest the deep breath of the wind, as of a woman who sighs deeply, may cast a panic into their hearts. Then some one rises in his stirrup and sees the spark of a lodging far off on the rim of the land. And if Our Lady is merciful to them they reach this in safety when we at home are on our knees in prayer for them.

(3)

My mother called me from my book this morning to talk with her in her room. I found her in the little chamber where my father is wont to sit, when he is at home, with the Manor Rolls and other legal papers before him. It is here that she sits when she has duty to do as the head of the household. I curtseyed deeply; thinking that I guessed already why she had sent for me.

She had a sheet spread before her, covered with close writing. She bade me read it; and then before I had taken the paper in my hand she cried, 'No – I will tell you myself.'

'Daughter,' she began, solemnly, 'it is high time that you were married. Indeed it is only the troubled state of the land' – she sighed – 'and our own perplexities, that have delayed the matter so long.'

'Do you think much of marriage?' she looked at me half smiling.

'I have no wish to leave you,' I said.

'Come, my child you speak like a Babe,' she laughed, though I think she was well pleased at my affection.

'And besides, if you married as I would have you marry' – she tapped the paper – 'you would not go far from me. You might for instance rule over the land of Kirflings – your land would touch ours – You would be our good neighbour. The Lord of Kirflings is Sir Amyas Bigod, a man of ancient name.'

'I think it is a suitable match; such as a mother might wish for her daughter,' she mused, always with the sheet before her.

As I have only seen Sir Amyas once, when he came home with my father from the sessions at Norwich, and as on that occasion my only speech with him was to invite him gravely to drink the sack which I proffered, curtseying, I could not pretend to add anything to what my mother said. All I knew was that he had a fair, straight face; and if his hair was gray, it was not so gray as my father's, and his land bordered ours so that we might well live happily together.

'Marriage, you must know my daughter,' went on my mother, 'is a great honour and a great burden. If you marry such a man as Sir Amyas you become not only the head of his household, and that is much, but the head of his race for ever and ever, and that is more. We will not talk of love – as that song writer of yours talks of love, as a passion and a fire and a madness.'

'O he is only a story teller, Mother,' I chimed in –

'And such things are not to be found in real life; at least I think not often.' My mother was used to consider gravely as she spoke.

'But that is beside the question. Here, my daughter,' and she spread the paper before her, 'is a writing from Sir Amyas, to your father; he asks for your hand, and wishes to know whether there are other treaties for you and what dowry we will give with you. He tells us what he will provide on his part. Now I give you this paper to read by yourself; that you may consider whether this exchange seems to you a fair one.'

I knew already what lands and monies I had as my portion; and I knew that as the only daughter of my father my dowry was no mean one.

So that I might continue in this country which I love, and might live on close to my mother, I would take less than my right both of wealth and of land. But the gravity of the compact is such that I felt as though several years were added to my age, when my mother handed me the roll of paper. Since I was a child, I have always heard my parents talk of my marriage; and during the last two or three years there have been several contracts almost made I know, that came to nothing in the end. I lose my youth however, and it is high time that a bargain were struck.

I thought, naturally, for a long time, until the dinner bell rung indeed at midday, of the general honour and burden, as my mother calls it, of marriage. No other event in the life of a woman can mean so great a change; for from flitting shadow like and unconsidered in her father's house, marriage suddenly forms her to a substantial body, with weight which people must see and make way for. That is of course, if her marriage is suitable. And so, every maiden waits this change with wonder and anxiety; for it will prove whether she is to be an honourable and authoritative woman for ever, like my mother; or it will show that she is of no weight or worth. Either in this world or in the next.

And if I marry well, the burden of a great name and of great lands will be on me; many servants will call me mistress; I shall be the mother of sons; in my husband's absence I shall rule his people, taking care for herds and crops and keeping watch on his enemies; within doors I shall store up fine linens and my chests shall be laden with spices and preserves; by the work of my needle all waste of time and use will be repaired and renewed so that at my death my daughter shall find her cupboards better lined with fine raiments than when I found them. And when I lie dead, the people from the countryside shall pass for three days before my body, praying and speaking good of me, and at the will of my children the priest shall say mass for my soul and candles shall burn in the church for ever and ever.

(4)

I was stopped in the midst of such reflections firstly by the dinner bell; and you must not be late, or you interfere with Sir John's grace and that means no pudding; and then, when I might have put myself more into the position of a married woman, Jeremy my brother, insisted that we should go for a walk with Anthony, my father's chief steward – after my mother that is.

He is a crass man, but I like him because he is a faithful servant, and knows as much about land and sheep as any man in Norfolk. It was he also who broke Lancelot's head in last Michaelmas for using bad language to my mother. He is for ever tramping our fields, and knows them better and loves them more, so I tell him, than any human creature. He is wedded to this clump of earth, and sees in it a thousand beauties and gifts such as ordinary men see in their wives. And, as we have trotted by his side since we could walk alone, some of his affection has become ours too; Norfolk and the parish of Long Winton in Norfolk is to me what my own grandmother is; a tender parent, dear and familiar, and silent to whom I shall return in time. O how blessed it would be never to marry, or grow old; but to spend one's life innocently and indifferently among the trees and rivers which alone can keep one cool and childlike in the midst of the troubles of the world! Marriage or any other great joy would confuse the clear vision which is still mine. And at the thought of losing that, I cried in my heart, 'No, I will never leave you – for a husband or a lover,' and straightway I started chasing rabbits across the heath with Jeremy and the dogs.

It was a cold afternoon, but a bright one; as though the sun were made of gleaming ice and not of fire; and its rays were long icicles that reached from sky to earth. They splintered on our cheeks, and went glancing across the fen. And the whole country seemed empty, save of a few swift rabbits, but very chaste and very glad in its solitude. We ran to keep warm, and chattered when the blood raced sparkling through our limbs. Anthony stalked straight on, as though his stride were the best thing in the world against the cold. Certainly when we came to a broken hedge, or a snare stretched for a rabbit, he took off his gloves and leant on his knee and took note of it as though it were a midsummer day. Once we came upon a strange man, slouching along the road, in rusty green, with the look of one who knows not which way to take. Anthony held my hand firmly; this was a Sanctuary man he said, prowling out of bounds in search of food. He had robbed or murdered, or perchance he was only a debtor. Jeremy swore he saw blood on his hands: but Jeremy is a boy, and would like to defend us all with his bow and arrows.

Anthony had some business at one of the cottages, and we came in with him out of the cold. But indeed, I could hardly stand the heat and the smell. Beatrice Somers, and her husband Peter live here, and they have children; but it was more like the burrow of some rabbit on the heath than the house of a man. Their roof was of brush, and straw, their floor was but the earth trodden bare of grass or flower; sticks burnt in the corner, and sent the smoke stinging into our eyes. There was but a rotten log on which a woman sat, nursing a baby. She looked at us, not with fright, but with distrust and dislike written clear in her eyes; and she clasped her child more closely. Anthony spoke to her as he would have spoken to some animal who had strong claws and a wicked eye: he stood over her, and his great boot seemed ready to crush her. But she did not move or speak; and

I doubt whether she could have spoken, or whether snarling and howling was her only language.

Outside we met Peter coming home from the fen, and tho' he touched his forehead to us, he seemed to have no more human sense in him than his wife. He looked at us, and seemed fascinated by a coloured cloak which I wore; and then he stumbled into his burrow, to lie on the ground I suppose, rolled in dried bracken till morning. These are the people we must rule; and tread under foot, and scourge them to do the only work they are fitted to do; as they will tear us to pieces with their fangs. Thus Anthony spoke as he took us away, and then clenched his fists and set his lips as though he were razing to the earth some such poor wretch already. Still the sight of that ugly face spoilt the rest of the walk; since it seemed that even my dear country bred pests like these. I saw such eyes staring at me from the furze bushes, and the tangles of the undergrowth.

It was like waking from a nightmare to enter our own clean hall, where the logs burnt tidily in the great chimney, and the oak shone bright; and my mother came down the staircase in her rich gown, with spotless linen on her head. But some of the lines on her face, and some of the sternness of her voice, had come there, I thought suddenly, because she always saw not far from her such sights as I had seen today.

(5)

May

The spring which has now reached us means more than the mere birth of green growing things; for once again the current of life which circles round England is melted from its winter frost, and in our little island we feel the tide chafing at our shores. For the last week or two strange wayfarers have been seen on the roads, who may be either pilgrims and pedlars, or gentlemen travelling in parties to London or the North. And at this season the mind becomes eager and hopeful even though the body must stay motionless. For as the evenings lengthen and new light seems to well up from the West so one may fancy that a new whiter light of another kind is spreading over the land; and you may feel it hitting your eyelids as you walk or sit over your embroidery.

In the midst of such a stir and tumult, one bright May morning, we saw the figure of a man striding along the road, walking fast and waving his arms as though he conversed with the air. He had a great wallet at his back and we saw that he held a stout book of parchment in one hand at which he glanced occasionally: and all the while he shouted words in a kind of measure with his feet, and his voice rose up and down, in menace or in plaint till Jeremy and I shrank close against the hedge. But he saw us; and pulled off his cap and made a deep bow; to which I curtseyed as properly as I could.

'Madam,' he said, in a voice that rolled like summer thunder, 'may I ask if this is the road to Long Winton?'

'It is only a mile in front of you, Sir,' I said, and Jeremy waved down the road with his stick.

'Then Sir,' he went on, shutting his book, and looking at once more sober and more conscious of the time and place, 'may I ask further where is the house where I could sell my books most easily? I am come all the way from Cornwall, singing songs, and trying to sell the manuscripts I have with me. My wallet is still full. The times are not favourable to songs.'

Indeed the man, though ruddy of cheek, and lusty of frame, was as ill dressed as any hind; and his boots were so patched that walking must have been a penance. But he had a kind of gaiety and courtesy about him, as though the fine music of his own songs clung to him and set him above ordinary thoughts.

I pulled my brother's arm, and said, 'We belong to the Hall ourselves Sir, and we will gladly shew you the way. I should be very glad to see those books of yours.' His eye lost its merriment at once; and he asked me almost sternly, 'Can you read?'

'O Joan's always got her nose in a book,' called out Jeremy, starting to talk, and pulling me too.

'Tell us about your travels Sir. Have you been to London? What is your name?'

'I am called Richard Sir,' said the man smiling. 'Doubtless I have another name, but I never heard it. I come from Gwithian which is in Cornwall; and I can sing you more Cornish songs, Madam, than any man in the Duchy.' He turned to me, and wound up with a flourish of one hand with the book in it. 'Here for instance – in this little volume, are all the stories of the Knights of the round Table; written out by the hand of Master Anthony himself, and painted by the Monks of Cam Brea. I value this more than my wife or children; for I have none; it is meat and drink to me, because I am given supper and lodging for singing the tales in it; it is horse and staff to me, for it has lifted me over many miles of weary road; and it is the best of all companions on the way; for it has always something new to sing me; and it will be silent when I wish to sleep. There never was such a book!'

Such was the way he talked, as I have never heard any man talk. For in speaking he did not seem to speak his mind exactly, or to care whether we understood him. But words seemed dear to him, whether he spoke them in jest or earnest. We reached our courtyard, and he straightened himself, flicked his boots with a handkerchief; and tried with many swift touches of his fingers to set his dress somewhat more in order than it was. Also he cleared his throat, as one preparing to sing. I ran to fetch my mother, who came slowly, and looked at him from an upper window before she would promise to hear him.

'His bag is stuffed with books, mother,' I urged; 'he has all the Tales of Arthur and the Round Table; I daresay he can tell us what became of Helen when her husband took her. O Mother, do let us hear him!'

She laughed at my impatience; but bade me call Sir John, for after all it was a fine morning.

When we came down the man Richard was walking up and down, discoursing to my brother of his travels; how he had knocked one man on the head, cried to the other, '"Come on Rascal" and the whole lot had fled like,' here he saw my mother, and swept off his hat as was his way.

'My daughter tells me Sir that you come from foreign parts, and can sing. We are but country people; and therefore I fear very little acquainted with the tales of other parts. But we are ready to listen. Sing us something of your land; and then, if you will, you shall sit down to meat with us, and we will gladly hear news of the country.'

She sat down on a bench beneath the oak tree; and Sir John came puffing to stand by her side. She bade Jeremy open the Gates, and let any of our people in who cared to hear. They came in shyly and curiously, and stood gaping at Master Richard, who once again waved his cap at them.

He stood on a small mound of grass; and began in a high melodious voice, to tell the story of Sir Tristram and the Lady Iseult.

He dropped his gay manner, and looked past us all, with straight fixed eyes, as though he drew his words from some sight not far from him. And as the story grew passionate his voice rose, and his fists clenched, and he raised his foot and stretched forth his arms; and then, when the lovers part, he seemed to see the Lady sink away from him, and his eye sought farther and farther till the vision was faded away; and his arms were empty. And then he is wounded in Brittany; and he hears the Princess coming across the seas to him.

But I cannot tell how it seemed that the air was full of Knights and Ladies, who passed among us, hand in hand, murmuring, and seeing us not; and then the poplars and the beech trees sent grey figures, with silver gems, floating down the air; and the morning was full, suddenly, of whispers, and sighs, and lovers' laments.

But then the voice stopped; and all these figures withdrew, fading and trailing across the sky to the West where they live. And when I opened my eyes, the man, and the grey wall; the people by the Gate, slowly swam up, as from some depths, and settled on the surface, and stayed there clear and cold.

'Poor things!' spoke my mother.

Meanwhile Richard was like a man who lets something slip from his clasp; and beats thin air. He looked at us, and I had half a mind to stretch out a hand; and tell him he was safe. But then he recollected himself, and smiled as though he had reason to be pleased.

He saw the crowd at the Gate; and struck up a jolly tune, about a Nut Brown Maid and her lover, and they grinned and stamped with their feet. Then my mother bade us come into dinner; and she sat Master Richard at her right side.

He eat like a man who has fed upon hips and haws, and drunk water from the brook. And after the meat had been taken away, he solemnly swung round his wallet; and took from it various things; which he laid upon the table. There were clasps and brooches, and necklaces of beads: but there were also many sheets of parchment stitched together; though none of such a size as his book. And then seeing my desire he placed the precious volume in my hands and bade me look at its pictures. Indeed it was a beautiful work; for the capital letters framed bright blue skies, and golden robes; and in the midst of the writing there came broad spaces of colour, in which you might see princes and princesses walking in procession and towns with churches upon steep hills, and the sea breaking blue beneath them. They were like little mirrors, held up to those visions which I had seen passing in the air but here they were caught and stayed for ever.

'And have you ever seen such sights as these?' I asked him.

'They are to be seen by those who look,' he answered mysteriously. And he took his manuscript from me, and tied the covers safely across it. He placed it in his breast.

It was as yellow and gnarled outside as the missal of any pious priest; but inside the brilliant knights and ladies moved, undimmed, to the unceasing melody of beautiful words. It was a fairy world that he shut inside his coat.

We offered him a night's lodging, nay more, if he would but stay and sing to us again. But he listened to our prayers no more than the owl in the ivy: saying merely, 'I must go on my way.' By dawn he was out of the house, and we felt as though some strange bird had rested on our roof for a moment, and flown on.

(6)

Midsummer

There comes a week, or may be it is only a day, when the year seems poised consciously on its topmost peak; it stays there motionless for a long or a short time, as though in majestic contemplation, and then slowly sinks like a monarch descending from his throne, and wraps itself round in darkness.

But figures are slippery things!

At this moment I have the feeling of one swung high into tranquil regions; upon the great back of the world. The peace of the nation, and the prosperity of our own small corner of it – for my father and brothers are at home – make a complete circle of satisfaction; you may pass from the smooth dome of sky, to our own roof without crossing my gulf.

Thus it seemed a most suitable time for our midsummer pilgrimage to the shrine of Our Lady at Walsingham; more especially as I have this year to give thanks for much, and to pray for more. My marriage with Sir Amyas is settled for the 20th day of December; and we are busy making ready. So yesterday I started at dawn, and travelled on foot in order to show that I approached the shrine with a humble spirit. And a good walk is surely the best preparation for prayers!

Start with your spirit fresh like a corn fed horse; let her rear and race, and bucket you hither and thither. Nothing will keep her to the road; and she will sport in dewy meadows, and crush a thousand delicate flowers beneath her feet.

But the day grows hot; and you may lead her, still with a springing step back to the straight way; and she will carry you lightly and swiftly, till the midday sun bids you rest. In sober truth, and without metaphor, the mind drives clearly through all the mazes of a stagnant spirit when a brisk pair of legs impells it; and the creature grows nimble, with its exercise. Thus I suppose I may have thought enough for a whole week lived indoors during those three hours that I spent striding along the road to Walsingham.

And my brain that was swift and merry at first, and leapt like a child at play, settled down in time to sober work upon the highway, though it was glad withal. For I thought of the serious things of life – such as age, and poverty and sickness and death, and considered that it would certainly be my lot to meet them; and I considered also those joys and sorrows that were for ever chasing themselves across my life. Small things would no longer please me or tease me as of old. But although this made me feel grave, I felt also that I had come to the time when such feelings are true; and further, as I walked, it seemed to me that one might enter within such feelings and study them, as, indeed, I had walked in a wide space within the covers of Master Richard's manuscript.

I saw them as solid globes of crystal; enclosing a round ball of coloured earth and air, in which tiny men and women laboured, as beneath the dome of the sky itself.

Walsingham, as all the world knows, is but a very small village on the top of a hill. But as you approach through a plain that is rich with green, you see this high ground rising above you for some time before you get there. The midday sun lit up all the soft greens and blues of the fen land; and made it seem as though one passed through a soft and luxurious land, glowing like a painted book; towards a stern summit, where the light struck upon something pointing upwards that was pale as bone.

At last I reached the top of the hill, joining with a stream of other pilgrims, and we clasped hands, to show that we came humbly as human beings and trod the last steps of the road together, singing our Miserere.

There were men and women, and lame people and blind people; and some were in rags, and some had ridden on horseback; I confess that my eyes sought their faces curiously, and I thought desperately for a moment that it was terrible that flesh and fens should divide us. They would have strange, merry stories to tell.

But then the pale cross with the Image struck my eyes, and drew all my mind, in reverence towards it.

I will not pretend that I found that summons other than stern; for the sun and storm have made the figure harsh and white; but the endeavour to adore Her as others were doing round me filled my mind with an image that was so large and white that no other thought had room there. For one moment I submitted myself to her as I have never submitted to man or woman, and bruised my lips on the rough stone of her garment. White light and heat steamed on my bare head; and when the ecstasy passed the country beneath flew out like a sudden banner unfurled.

(7)

Autumn

The Autumn comes; and my marriage is not far off. Sir Amyas is a good gentleman, who treats me with great courtesy and hopes to make me happy. No poet could sing of our courtship; and, I must confess that since I have taken to reading of Princesses, I have sometimes grieved that my own lot was so little like theirs. But then they did not live in Norfolk, at the time of the Civil Wars; and my mother tells me that the truth is always finest.

To prepare me for my duties as a married woman, she has let me help her in the management of the house and lands; and I begin to understand how much of my time will be passed in thoughts which have nothing to do with men or with happiness. There are the sheep, the woods, the crops, the people, things all needing my care and judgment when my Lord is away as he will be so often; and if times are as troubled as they have been, I must also act as chief Lieutenant in the disposition of his forces against the enemy. And then there will be my proper work as a woman calling me within the house. Truly, as my mother says, there will be little time for Princes and Princesses! And she went on to expound to me what she calls her theory of ownership; how, in these times, one is as the Ruler of a small island set in the midst of turbulent waters; how one must plant it and culti-vate it; and drive roads through it, and fence it securely from the tides; and one day perhaps the waters will abate and this plot of ground will be ready to make part of a new world. Such is her dream of what the future may bring to England; and it has been the hope of her life to order her own province in such a way that it may make one firm spot of ground to tread on at any rate. She bids me hope that I may live to see the whole of England thus solidly established; and if I do, I shall thank my mother, and other women like her.

But I confess that deeply though I honour my mother and respect her words, I cannot accept their wisdom without a sigh. She seems to look forward to nothing better than an earth rising solid out of the mists that now enwreathe it; and the fairest prospect in her mind is, I believe, a broad road running through the land, on which she sees long strings of horsemen, riding at their ease, pilgrims stepping cheerily unarmed, and waggons that pass each other going laden to the coast and returning as heavily laden with goods taken from ships. Then she would dream of certain great houses, lying open to the sight, with their moats filled up and their towers pulled down; and the gate would open freely to any passer by; and there would be cheer for guest or serving man at the same table with the Lord. And you would ride through fields brimming with corn, and there would be flocks and herds in all the pasture lands and cottages of stone for the poor. As I write this down, I see that it is good; and we should do right to wish it.

But at the same time, when I imagine such a picture, painted before me, I cannot think it pleasant to look upon; and I fancy that I should find it hard to draw my breath upon those smooth bright ways.

Yet what it is that I want, I cannot tell, although I crave for it, and in some secret way, expect it. For often, and oftener as time goes by, I find myself suddenly halting in my walk, as though I were stopped by a strange new look upon the surface of the land which I know so well. It hints at something; but it is gone before I know what it means. It is as though a new smile crept out of a well known face; it half frightens you, and yet it beckons.

Last Pages

My father came in yesterday when I was sitting before the desk at which I write these sheets. He is not a little proud of my skill in reading and writing; which indeed I have learnt mostly at his knee.

But confusion came over me when he asked me what I wrote; and stammering that it was a 'Diary' I covered the pages with my hands.

'Ah,' he cried, 'if my father had only kept a diary! But he, poor man, could not write his own name even. There's John and Pierce and Stephen all lying in the church yonder, and no word left to say whether they were good men or bad.' Thus he spoke till my cheeks were pale again.

'And so my grandson will say of me,' he went on. 'And if I could I should like to write a line myself: to say "I am Giles Martyn; I am a middle sized man, dark skinned, hazel eyed, with hair on my lip; I can read and write, but none too easy. I ride to London on as good a bay mare as is to be found in the County."'

'Well what more should I say? And would they care to hear it? And who will *they* be?' he laughed; for it was his temper to end his speech with a laugh, even though he began it soberly.

'You would like to hear of your father,' I said; 'why shouldn't they care to hear of you?'

'My fathers were much as I am;' he said; 'they lived here, all of 'em; they ploughed the same land that I plough; they married women from the countryside. Why they might walk in at the door this moment, and I should know 'em, and should think it nothing strange. But the future' – he spread out his hands – 'who can tell? We may be washed off the face of the earth, Joan.'

'Oh no,' I cried; 'I am certain we shall live here always.' This pleased my father secretly; for there is no man who cares more for his land and his name than he does; though he will always hold that had we been a prouder race, we should not have stayed so long in the same prosperity.

'Well then Joan, you must keep your writing,' he said; 'or rather, I must keep it for you. For you are going to leave us – not to go far though,' he added quickly; 'and names matter but little. Still, I should like to have some token of you when you are away; and our descendants shall have cause to respect one of us at least.' He looked with great admiration at the neat lines of my penmanship. 'Now my girl, come with me, to the Church, where I must see to the carving on my father's tomb.'

As I walked with him, I thought of his words and of the many sheets that lie written in my oaken desk. Winter had come round again since I made my first flourish so proudly. Thinking that there were few women in Norfolk who could do the like; and were it not that some such pride stayed with me I think that my writing would have ceased long before this. For, truly, there is nothing in the pale of my days that needs telling; and the record grows wearisome. And I thought as I went along in the sharp air of the winter morning, that if I ever write again it shall not be of Norfolk and myself, but of Knights and ladies and of adventures in strange lands. The clouds even, which roll up from the west and advance across the sky take the likeness of Captains and of soldiery and I can scarcely cease from fashioning helmets and swords, as well as fair faces, and high headdresses from these waves of coloured mist.

But as my mother would say, the best of stories are those that are told over the fire side; and I shall be well content if I may end my days as one of those old women who can keep a household still on a winter's evening, with her tales of the strange sights that she saw and the deeds that were done in her youth. I have always thought that such stories came partly out of the clouds, or why should they stir us more than any thing we can see for ourselves? It is certain that no written book can stand beside them.

Such a woman was Dame Elsbeth Aske, who, when she grew too old to knit or stitch and too stiff to leave her chair, sat with clasped hands by the fire all day long, and you had only to pull her sleeve and her eyes grew bright, and she would tell you stories of fights and kings, and great nobles, and stories of the poor people too, till the air seemed to move and murmur. She could sing ballads also; which she made as she sat there. And men and women, old and young, came long distances to hear her; for all that she could neither write nor read. And they thought that she could tell the future too.

Thus we came to the church where my fathers lie buried. The famous stone Carver, Ralph of Norwich, has lately wrought a tomb for my grandfather, and it lies almost finished now, above his body; and the candles were flaring upright in the dim church when we entered. We knelt and whispered prayers for his soul; and then my father withdrew in talk with Sir John; and left me to my favourite task of spelling out the names and gazing down at the features of my dead kinsmen and ancestors. As a child I know the stark white figures used to frighten me; especially when I could read that they bore my name; but now that I know that they never move from their backs, and keep their hands crossed always, I pity them; and would fain do some small act that would give them pleasure. It must be something secret, and unthought of – a kiss or a stroke, such as you give a living person.

A Dialogue upon
Mount Pentelicus

It so happened not many weeks ago that a party of English tourists was descending the slopes of Mount Pentelicus. Now they would have been the first to correct that sentence and to point out how much inaccuracy and indeed injustice was contained in such a description of themselves. For to call a man a tourist when you meet him abroad is to define not only his circumstance but his soul; and their souls they would have said – but the donkeys stumble so on the stones – were subject to no such limitation. Germans are tourists and Frenchmen are tourists but Englishmen are Greeks. Such was the sense of their discourse, and we must take their word for it that it was very good sense indeed.

Mount Pentelicus, as we who read Baedeker know, yet bears on her side the noble scar that she suffered at the hands of certain Greek stone masons who had the smile and perhaps the curse of Pheidias as their reward of their labour.[5] And so if you would do justice to her you must meditate on several separate themes and combine them as best you may. You must think of her not only as the outline that ran across many Greek casements – Plato looked up from his page on sunny mornings – but also as the workshop and as the living place where innumerable slaves wore out their lives. And it was salutary when at midday the party dismounted, to stumble painfully among the crude blocks of marble, which for some reason had been overlooked or cast aside when the carts went down the hill to Athens. It was salutary, because in Greece it is possible to forget that statues are made of marble, and it was wholesome to see that marble opposes itself, solid and sharp and perverse to the sculptor's chisel.

'Such were the Greeks!' And if you had heard that cry you would have supposed that each speaker had some personal conquest to celebrate and was the generous victor of the stone himself. He had forced it to yield its Hermes or its Apollo once with his own hands. But then the donkeys, whose ancestors had been stabled in the grotto put an end to meditation and the riders, six of them in order, stepped gravely down the hill side. They had seen Marathon and Salamis and Athens would have been theirs too had not a cloud caressed it; at any rate they felt themselves charged on each side by tremendous presences. And to prove themselves duly inspired, they not only shared their wine flask with the escort of dirty Greek peasant boys but condescended so far as to address them in their own tongue as Plato would have spoken it had Plato learned Greek at Harrow. Whether they were just or not shall be left for others to decide; but the fact that Greek words spoken on Greek soil were misunderstood by Greeks destroys at one blow the whole population of Greece, both men and women and children. At such a crisis one word came aptly to their lips; a word that Sophocles might have spoken, and that Plato would have sanctioned; they were 'barbarians'. To denounce them thus was not only to discharge a duty on behalf of the dead but to declare the rightful inheritors, and for some minutes the marble quarries of Pentelicus thundered the news to all who might sleep beneath their rocks or haunt their caverns. The spurious people was convicted; the dusky garrulous race, loose of lip and unstable of purpose who had parodied the speech and pilfered the name of the great for so long was caught and convicted. Obedient to the cry the muleteer came down upon the quarters of his charge – a white mule led the file – with the good will of one who saves his own back each blow that he lays upon another's. For when the English shouted he judged that it was best to go faster. Nor could he have proved himself a happier critic; the moment had its word; no poet could do more; a prose writer might easily have done less. So with that single shout the English tumbled loosely from their climax and rattled down the mountain side as careless and as jocund as though the land were theirs.

But the descent of Pentelicus is stayed by a flat green ledge where nature seems to stand upright for a moment before she plunges down the hill again. There are great plane trees spreading benevolent hands, and there are comfortable little bushes ranged in close domestic order, and there is a stream which may be thought to sing their praises and the delights of wine and song. You might have heard the voice of Theocritus[6] in the plaint that it made on the stones, and certain of the English did so hear it, albeit the text was dusty on their shelves at home. Here at any rate nature and the chant of the classic spirit prompted the six friends to dismount and rest themselves. Their guides withdrew, yet not so far but that they could be seen at their barbarian antics, rolling and singing, pulling each other by the sleeve and chattering of the vintage that now hung purple in the fields. But if there is one thing that we know about the Greeks it is that they were a still people, significant of gesture and speech, and when they sat down by the stream beneath the plane tree they disposed themselves as the vase painter would have chosen to depict them: the old man propped his chin on his staff so that his brow bent dark above the youth who lay upon the grass at his feet. And grave women in white draperies passed behind, silent, with pitchers balanced on their shoulders. No scholar in Europe could have rearranged that picture, or convinced our friends that any had a better right to construct such visions than themselves.

They stretched themselves then in the shade, and it was no fault of theirs or of the ancients if their discourse fell short in design at least of its noble model. But since dialogues are even more hard to write than to speak, and it is doubtful whether written dialogues have ever been spoken or spoken dialogues have ever been written, we will only rescue such fragments as concern our story. But this we will say, that the talk was the finest talk in the world.

It ranged over many subjects – over birds and foxes, and whether turpentine is good in wine – how the ancients made cheese – the position of women in the Greek state – that was eloquent! – the metres of Sophocles – the saddling of donkeys: and so sinking and surging like the flight of an eagle through mid-air it dropped at last upon the tough old riddle of the modern Greek and his position in the world today. Some, of optimistic nature, claimed for him a present, some less credulous but still sanguine expected a future, and others with generous imagination recalled a past; but it was left for one to combat all these superstitions as he struck at the stump of a withered olive tree, and to demonstrate with great shocks of speech and of muscle what it was that the Greeks had been, and what it is that they are no longer.

Such a people he said – and as he spoke the sun was in the sky, and a golden eagle hung above the hill – such a people were as sudden as the dawn, and died as the day dies here in Greece, completely. Ignorant of all that should be ignored – of charity, religion, domestic life, learning and science – they fixed their minds upon the beautiful and the good, and found them sufficient not for this world only but for an infinite number of worlds to come. 'Where the Greeks had modesty –' but to finish the quotation, for he must read what none now could speak, he called for his Peacock,[7] and his Peacock had been left with certain socks and a tin of tobacco, the bitterest loss of all, in the ruins of Olympia, and he was forced to take up the strain a little lower down in the scale though with no less earnestness than he began it. He said then how the Greeks by paring down the superfluous had revealed at last the perfect statue, or the sufficient stanza, just as we obversely by cloaking them in our rags of sentiment and imagination had obscured the outline and destroyed the substance. Look he exclaimed, upon the Apollo at Olympia, upon the head of a boy in Athens, read the *Antigone*,[8] stroll among the ruins of the Parthenon, and ask yourself whether there is room at the side or at the foot for any later form of beauty to creep in. Rather is it not true, as fancy hints in the dark and the pallid dawn, that just so many shapes of beauty swam in the vague for thought to realise as the Greeks circled with stone and with language, and that nothing is left for us but to worship in silence or if we choose, to churn the empty air?

One answered him, whose character was already spotted with a dangerous heresy; for only a year ago he had made use of a brand new vote to affirm that Greek should cease as he put it, 'to whip stupid boys into good behaviour.' And yet he was a scholar. His argument, but we must beware of the dialogue, was something of this sort, save for certain interruptions which no rearrangement of the alphabet will convey.

'When you talk of the Greeks,' he said, 'you speak as a sentimentalist and a sloven, and you are very fond of talking of the Greeks. It is no wonder that you love them, for they represent, as you have been saying, all that is noble in art and true in philosophy, and as you might have added all that is best in yourself. Certainly there never was a people like them; and the reason why you – who took a third in your tripos, you may remember – call them the Greeks is because it seems to you impious to call them the Italians or the French or the Germans, or by the name of any people indeed who can build bigger fleets than ours or talk a language that we can understand. No, let us give them a name which can be spelt in different ways, which can be given to different peoples, which etymologists can define, which archaeologists can dispute, which can mean in short all that we do not know and as in your case all that we dream and desire. Indeed there is no reason why you should read their writings, for have you not written them? Their mystic and secret pages embalm all that you have felt to be beautiful in art and true in philosophy. For there is, you know, a soul of beauty that rises unchristened over the words of Milton as it rises over the Bay of Marathon yonder; perchance it may slip us and fade, for we distrust phantoms. But you I doubt not are busy even at this moment baptising it with a Greek name, and enclosing it in a Greek shape. Is it not already that "something in the Greek" which you never read there; and part – the best part – of Sophocles and Plato and all those dark books at home? So, while you read your Greek on the slopes of Pentelicus, you deny that her children exist any longer. But for us scholars –'

'O ignorant and illogical' interrupted the answer, and so might have continued to the end of the paragraph but that another reply was vouchsafed which seemed conclusive at the moment though it did not proceed from Heaven but only from the hill side. The little bushes creaked and bent, and a great brown form surged out of them, his head obscured by the bundle of dried wood that he carried on his shoulders. At first there was some hope that he might be a fine specimen of the European bear, but a second glance proved that he was only a monk discharging the humble duties of the monastery near by. He did not see the six Englishmen till he was close up to them, and then their presence made him stand erect and gaze as though startled against his will from pleasant meditations. So they saw that he was large and finely made, and had the nose and brow of a Greek statue. It was true that he wore a beard and his hair was long, and there was every reason to think him both dirty and illiterate. But as he stood there, suspended, with open eyes, a fantastic – a pathetic – hope shot through the minds of some who saw him that his was one of those original figures which, dipped in the crude earth, have resisted time, and recall the first days and the unobliterated type: there might be such a thing as Man.

But it is no longer within the power of the English mind – the gift may be enjoyed perhaps in Russia – to see fur grow upon smooth ears and cloven hoofs where there are ten separate toes. It is their power to see something different from that, and perhaps, who knows?, something finer. At any rate the six English stretched beneath the plane tree felt themselves first of all compelled to draw in their untidy limbs and then to sit erect and then to return the gaze of the brown monk as one man gazes at another. Such was the force of the eye that fixed them, for it was not only clarified by the breeze among the olive groves but it was lit by another power which survives trees and even plants them. And certainly, interpret it how you will, whether you tell it as a fact or whisper it as a miracle, and it may be both, the light was such that it made the trees murmur and the air blow. And thousands of little creatures moved about in the grass, and the earth turned solid for miles and miles beneath the feet. Nor did the atmosphere begin and end with that day and that horizon, but it stretched like a lucid green river on all sides immeasurably and the world swam in its girdle of eternity. Such was the light in the brown monk's eye, and to think of death or dust or destruction beneath its gaze was like placing a sheet of tissue paper in the fire. For it pierced through much, and went like an arrow drawing a golden chain through ages and races till the shapes of men and women and the sky and the trees rose up on either side of its passage and stretched in a solid and continuous avenue from one end of time to the other.

And the English could not have told at the moment at which point they stood, for the avenue was as smooth as a ring of gold. But the Greeks, that is Plato and Sophocles and the rest, were close to them, as close to them as any friend or lover, and breathed the same air as that which kissed the cheek and stirred the vine, only like young people they still pressed in front and questioned the future. Such a flame as that in the monk's eye, though it had wandered in obscure places since, and had shone upon the barren hill side and among the stones and the stunted little trees, had been lit once at the original hearth; and, doubt-less it will burn on still in the head of monk or peasant when more ages are passed than the brain can number.

All that the brown monk said however was καλησπέρα, which is good evening, and it was odd that he addressed the gentleman who had been the first to proclaim the doom of his race. And as he returned the salutation, rising to do so and taking the pipe from his lips, the conviction was his that he spoke as a Greek to a Greek and if Cambridge disavowed the relationship the slopes of Pentelicus and the olive groves of Mendeli confirmed it.

But the dusk that cuts short the Grecian day was falling like a knife across the sky; and as they rode home along the high way between the vines the lights were opening in the streets of Athens and the talk was of supper and a bed.

Memoirs of a Novelist

When Miss Willatt died, in October 1884, it was felt, as her biographer puts it, 'that the world had a right to know more of an admirable though retiring woman'. From the choice of adjectives it is clear that she would not have wished it herself unless one could have convinced her that the world would be the gainer. Perhaps, before she died, Miss Linsett did convince her, for the two volumes of life and letters which that lady issued were produced with the sanction of the family. If one chose to take the introductory phrase and moralise upon it one might ask a page full of interesting questions. What right has the world to know about men and women? What can a biographer tell it? and then, in what sense can it be said that the world profits? The objection to asking these questions is not only that they take so much room, but that they lead to an uncomfortable vagueness of mind. Our conception of the world is that it is a round ball, coloured green where there are fields and forests, wrinkled blue where there is sea, with little peaks pinched up upon it, where there are mountain ranges. When we are asked to imagine the effect of Miss Willatt or another upon this object, the enquiry is respectful but without animation. Yet, if it would be a waste of time to begin at the beginning and ask why lives are written, it may not be entirely without interest to ask why the life of Miss Willatt was written, and so to answer the question, who she was.

Miss Linsett, although she cloaked her motives under large phrases, had some stronger impulse at the back of her. When Miss Willatt died, 'after fourteen years of unbroken friendship', Miss Linsett (if we may theorise) felt uneasy. It seemed to her that if she did not speak at once something would be lost. At the same time no doubt other thoughts pressed upon her; how pleasant mere writing is, how important and unreal people become in print so that it is a credit to have known them; how one's own figure can have justice done to it – but the first feeling was the most genuine. When she looked out of the window as she drove back from the funeral, she felt first that it was strange, and then that it was unseemly, that the people in the street should pass, whistling some of them, and all of them looking indifferent. Then, naturally, she had letters from 'mutual friends'; the editor of a newspaper asked her to write an appreciation in a thousand words; and at last she suggested to Mr William Willatt that someone ought to write his sister's life. He was a solicitor, with no literary experience, but did not object to other people's writing so long as they did not 'break down the barriers'; in short Miss Linsett wrote the book which one may still buy with luck in the Charing Cross Road.

It does not seem, to judge by appearances, that the world has so far made use of its right to know about Miss Willatt. The volumes had got themselves wedged between Sturm 'On the Beauties of Nature' and the 'Veterinary Surgeon's Manual' on the outside shelf, where the gas cracks and the dust grimes them, and people may read so long as the boy lets them. Almost unconsciously one begins to confuse Miss Willatt with her remains and to condescend a little to these shabby, slipshod volumes. One has to repeat that she did live once, and it would be more to the purpose could one see what she was like then than to say (although it is true) that she is slightly ridiculous now.

Who was Miss Willatt then? It is likely that her name is scarcely known to the present generation; it is a mere chance whether one has read any of her books. They lie with the three-volume novels of the sixties and the seventies upon the topmost shelves of little seaside libraries, so that one has to take a ladder to reach them, and a cloth to wipe off the dust.

She was born in 1823, and was the daughter of a solicitor in Wales. They lived for part of the year near Tenby, where her father had his office, and she 'came out' at a ball given by the officers of the local Masonic Guild in the Town Hall, at Pembroke. Although Miss Linsett takes thirty-six pages to cover these seventeen years, she hardly mentions them. True, she tells us how the Willatts were descended from a merchant in the sixteenth century, who spelt his name with a V; and how Frances Ann, the novelist, had two uncles, one of whom invented a new way of washing sheep, and the other 'will long be remembered by his parishioners. It is said that even the very poorest wore some piece of mourning... in memory of "the good Parson".' But these are merely biographer's tricks – a way of marking time, during those chill early pages when the hero will neither do nor say anything 'characteristic'. For some reason we are told little of Mrs Willatt, daughter of Mr Josiah Bond, a respected linendraper, who, at a later date seems to have bought 'a place'. She died when her only daughter was sixteen; there were two sons, Frederic, who died before his sister, and William, the solicitor, who survived her. It is perhaps worth while to say these things, although they are ugly and no one will remember them, because they help us somehow to believe in the otherwise visionary youth of our heroine. When Miss Linsett is forced to talk of her and not of her uncles, this is the result. 'Frances, thus, at the age of sixteen, was left without a mother's care. We can imagine how the lonely girl, for even the loving companionship of father and brothers could not fill *that* place [but we know nothing about Mrs Willatt][9] sought for consolation in solitude, and, wandering among the heaths and dunes where the castles of an earlier age are left to crumble into ruins, &c &c.' Mr William Willatt's contribution to his sister's biography is surely more to the purpose. 'My sister was a shy awkward girl, much given to "mooning". It was a standing joke in the family that she had once walked into the pigsty, mistaking it for the wash house, and had not discovered her whereabouts until Grunter (the old black sow) ate her book out of her hands. With reference to her studious habits, I should say that these were always very marked... I may mention the fact that any act of disobedience was most effectually punished by the confiscation of her bedroom candle, by the light of which it was her habit to read in bed. I well remember, as a small boy, the look of my sister's figure as she leant out of bed, book in hand, so as to get the benefit of the chink of light which came through the door from the other room where our nurse was sewing. In this way she read the whole of Bright's history of the Church, always a favourite book with her. I am afraid that we did not always treat her studies with respect... She was not generally considered handsome, although she had (at the date of which I speak) a nearly perfect arm.' With respect to this last remark, an important one, we can consult the likeness which some local artist made of Miss Willatt at the age of seventeen. It needs no insight to affirm that it is not a face that would have found favour in the Pembroke Town Hall in 1840. A heavy plait of hair, (which the artist has made to shine) coils round the brow; she has large eyes, but they are slightly prominent; the lips are full, without being sensuous; the one feature which, when comparing her face with the faces of her friends, generally gave her courage, is the nose; perhaps someone had said in her hearing that it was a fine nose – a bold nose for a woman to have; at any rate her portraits, with one exception, are in profile.

We can imagine (to steal Miss Linsett's useful phrase) that this 'shy awkward girl much given to mooning' who walked in to pigsties, and read history instead of fiction, did not enjoy her first ball. Her brother's words evidently sum up what was in the air as they drove home. She found some angle in the great ball room where she could half hide her large figure, and there she waited to be asked to dance. She fixed her eyes upon the festoons which draped the city arms and tried to fancy that she sat on a rock with the bees humming round her; she bethought her how no one in that room perhaps knew as well as she did what was meant by the Oath of Uniformity; then she thought how in sixty years, or less perhaps, the worm would feed upon them all; then she wondered whether somehow before that day, every man now dancing there would not have reason to respect her. She wrote to Miss Ellen Buckle, to whom all her early letters are addressed, that 'disappointment is mixed with our pleasures, wisely enough, so that we may not forget &c &c'. And yet, it is likely that among all that company who danced in the Town Hall and are now fed on by the worm, Miss Willatt would have been the best to talk to, even if one did not wish to dance with her. Her face is heavy, but it is intelligent.

This impression is on the whole borne out by her letters. 'It is now ten o'clock, and I have come up to bed; but I shall write to you first... It has been a heavy but I trust not an unprofitable day... Ah, my dearest friend, for you are dearest, how should I bear the secrets of my soul and the weight of what the poet calls this "unintelligible world"[10] without you to impart them to?' One must brush aside a great deal of tarnished compliment, and then one gets a little further into Miss Willatt's mind. Until she was eighteen or so she had not realised that she had any relationship to the world; with self-consciousness came the need of settling the matter, and, consequently, a terrible depression. Without more knowledge than Miss Willatt gives us, we can only guess how she came by her conceptions of human nature and right and wrong. From histories she got a general notion of pride, avarice and bigotry; in the Waverley novels[11] she read about love. These ideas vaguely troubled her. Lent religious works by Miss Buckle, she learnt, with relief, how one may escape the world, and at the same time earn everlasting joy. There was never to be a greater saint than she was, by the simple device of saying, before she spoke or acted, is this right? The world then was very hideous, for the uglier she found it the more virtuous she became. 'Death was in that house, and Hell yawned before it,' she wrote, having passed, one evening, a room with crimson windows and heard the voices of dancers within; but the sensations with which she wrote were not entirely painful. Nevertheless her seriousness only half protected her, and left space for innumerable torments. 'Am I the only blot upon the face of nature?' she asked in May, 1841. 'The birds are carolling outside my windows, the very insects are putting off the winter's dross.' She alone was 'heavy as unleavened bread'. A terrible self-consciousness possessed her, and she writes to Miss Buckle as though she watched her shadow trembling over the entire world, beneath the critical eyes of the angels. It was humped and crooked and swollen with evil, and it taxed the powers of both the young women to put it straight. 'What would I not give to help you?' writes Miss Buckle. Our difficulty as we read now is to understand what their aim was; for it is clear that they imagined a state in which the soul lay tranquil and in bliss, and that if one could reach it one was perfect. Was it beauty that they were feeling for? As, at present, neither of them had any interest except in virtue, it is possible that aesthetic pleasure disguised had part in their religion. When they lay in these trances they were at any rate out of their surroundings. But the only pleasure that they allowed themselves to feel was the pleasure of submission.

Here, unfortunately, we come to an abyss. Ellen Buckle, as was likely, for she was less disgusted with the world than her friend and more capable of shifting her burdens on to human shoulders, married an engineer by whom her doubts were set at rest for ever. At the same time Frances had a strange experience of her own, which is concealed by Miss Linsett, in the most provoking manner conceivable, in the following passage. 'No one who has read the book (*Life's Crucifix*) can doubt that the heart which conceived the sorrows of Ethel Eden in her unhappy attachment had felt some of the pangs so feelingly described itself; so much we may say, more we may not.' The most interesting event in Miss Willatt's life, owing to the nervous prudery and the dreary literary conventions of her friend, is thus a blank. Naturally, one believes that she loved, hoped and saw her hopes extinguished, but what happened and what she felt we must guess. Her letters at this time are incurably dull, but that is partly because the word love and whole passages polluted by it, have shrunk into asterisks. There is no more talk of unworthiness and 'O might I find a retreat from the world I would then consider myself blessed'; death disappears altogether; she seems to have entered upon the second stage of her development, when, theories absorbed or brushed aside, she sought only to preserve herself. Her father's death, in 1855, is made to end a chapter, and her removal to London, where she kept house for her brothers in a Bloomsbury Square begins the next one.

At this point we can no longer disregard what has been hinted several times; it is clear that one must abandon Miss Linsett altogether, or take the greatest liberties with her text. What with 'a short sketch of the history of Bloomsbury may not be amiss', accounts of charitable societies and their heroes, a chapter upon Royal visits to the hospital, praise of Florence Nightingale in the Crimea, we see only a wax work as it were of Miss Willatt preserved under glass. One is just on the point of shutting up the book for ever, when a reflection bids one pause; the whole affair is, after all, extraordinarily odd. It seems incredible that human beings should think that these things are true of each other, and if not, that they should take the trouble to say them. 'She was justly esteemed for her benevolence, and her strict uprightness of character, which however never brought upon her the reproach of hardness of heart... She was fond of children animals and the spring, and Wordsworth was among her "bedside poets"... Although she felt his (her father's) death with the tenderness of a devoted daughter, she did not give way to useless and therefore selfish repining.... The poor, it might be said, took the place to her of her own children.' To pick out such phrases is an easy way of satirising them, but the steady drone of the book in which they are imbedded makes satire an afterthought; it is the fact that Miss Linsett believed these things and not the absurdity of them that dismays one. She believed at any rate that one should admire such virtues and attribute them to one's friends both for their sake and for one's own; to read her therefore is to leave the world in daylight, and to enter a closed room, hung with claret coloured plush, and illustrated with texts. It would be interesting to discover what prompted this curious view of human life, but it is hard enough to rid Miss Willatt of her friend's disguises without enquiring where she found them. Happily there are signs that Miss Willatt was not what she seemed. They creep out in the notes, in her letters, and most clearly in her portraits. The sight of that large selfish face, with the capable forehead and the surly but intelligent eyes, discredits all the platitudes on the opposite page; she looks quite capable of having deceived Miss Linsett.

When her father died (she had always disliked him) her spirits rose, and she determined to find scope for the 'great powers of which I am conscious' in London. Living in a poor neighbour-hood, the obvious profession for a woman in those days was to do good; and Miss Willatt devoted herself at first with exemplary vigour. Because she was unmarried she set herself to represent the unsentimental side of the community; if other women brought children into the world, she would do something for their health. She was in the habit of checking her spiritual progress, and casting up her accounts in the blank pages at the end of her diary, where one notes one's weight, and height and the number of one's watch; and she has often to rebuke her 'unstable spirit that is always seeking to distract me, and asking Whither?' Perhaps therefore she was not so well content with her philanthropy as Miss Linsett would have us believe. 'Do I know what happiness is?' she asks in 1859, with rare candour, and answers after thinking it over, 'No.' To imagine her then, as the sleek sober woman that her friend paints her, doing good wearily but with steadfast faith, is quite untrue; on the contrary she was a restless and discontented woman, who sought her own happiness rather than other people's. It was then that she bethought her of literature, taking the pen in hand, at the age of thirty-six, more to justify her complicated spiritual state than to say what must be said. It is clear that her state was complicated, even if we hesitate, remote as we are, to define it. She found at any rate that she had 'no vocation' for philanthropy, and told the Rev. R.S. Rogers so in an interview 'that was painful and agitating to us both' on February the 14th, 1856. But, in owning that, she admitted that she was without many virtues, and it was necessary to prove, to herself at least, that she had others. After all, merely to sit with your eyes open fills the brain, and perhaps in emptying it, one may come across something illuminating. George Eliot and Charlotte Bronte between them must share the parentage of many novels at this period, for they disclosed the secret that the precious stuff of which books are made lies all about one, in drawing-rooms and kitchens where women live, and accumulates with every tick of the clock.

Miss Willatt adopted the theory that no training is necessary, but thought it indecent to describe what she had seen, so that instead of a portrait of her brothers (and one had led a very queer life) or a memory of her father (for which we should have been grateful) she invented Arabian lovers and set them on the banks of the Orinoco. She made them live in an ideal community, for she enjoyed framing laws, and the scenery was tropical, because one gets one's effects quicker there than in England. She could write pages about 'mountains that looked like ramparts of cloud, save for the deep blue ravines that cleft their sides, and the diamond cascades that went leaping and flashing, now golden, now purple, as they entered the shade of the pine forests and passed out into the sun, to lose themselves in a myriad of streams upon the flower enamelled pasturage at their base'. But when she had to face her lovers, and the talk of the women in the tents at sundown when the goats came in to be milked, and the wisdom of 'that sage old man who had witnessed too many births and deaths to rejoice at the one or lament at the other' then she stammered and blushed perceptibly. She could not say 'I love you,' but used 'thee' and 'thou', which, with their indirectness, seemed to hint that she was not committing herself. The same self-consciousness made it impossible for her to think herself the Arab or his bride, or anyone indeed except the portentous voice that linked the dialogues, and explained how the same temptations assail us under the tropical stars and beneath the umbrageous elms of England.

For these reasons the book is now scarcely to be read through, and Miss Willatt also had scruples about writing well. There was something shifty, she thought, in choosing one's expressions; the straightforward way to write was the best, speaking out everything in one's mind, like a child at its mother's knee, and trusting that, as a reward, some meaning would be included. Nevertheless her book went into two editions, one critic likening it to the novels of George Eliot, save that the tone was 'more satisfactory', and another proclaiming that it was 'the work of Miss Martineau[12] or the Devil'.

If Miss Linsett were still alive (she died in Australia however, some years ago) one would like to ask her upon what system she cut her friend's life into chapters. They seem, when possible, to depend upon changes of address, and confirm us in our belief that Miss Linsett had no other guide to Miss Willatt's character. The great change came, surely, after the publication of *Lindamara: a Fantasy*. When Miss Willatt had her memorable 'scene' with Mr

Rogers she was so much agitated that she walked twice round Bedford Square, with the tears sticking her veil to her face. It seemed to her that all this talk of philanthropy was great nonsense, and gave one no chance of 'an individual life' as she called it. She had thoughts of emigrating, and founding a society, in which she saw herself, by the time she had finished her second round, with white hair, reading wisdom from a book to a circle of industrious disciples, who were very like the people she knew, but called her by a word that is a euphemism for 'Mother'. There are passages in *Lindamara* which hint at it, and allude covertly to Mr Rogers – 'the man in whom wisdom was not'. But she was indolent, and praise made her plausible; it came from the wrong people. The best of her writing – for we have dipped into several books, and the results seem to square with our theory – was done to justify herself, but, having accomplished that, she went on to prophesy for others, dwelling in vague regions with great damage to her system. She grew enormously stout, 'a symptom of disease' says Miss Linsett, who loved that mournful subject – a symptom to us of tea parties in her hot little drawing-room with the spotted wall paper, and of intimate conversations about 'the Soul'. 'The Soul' became her province, and she deserted the Southern plains for a strange country draped in eternal twilight, where there are qualities without bodies. Thus, Miss Linsett being at the time in great despondency about life, 'the death of an adored parent having deprived me of all my earthly hope', she went to see Miss Willatt, and left her flushed and tremulous, but convinced that she knew a secret that explained everything. Miss Willatt was far too clever to believe that anyone could answer anything; but the sight of these queer little trembling women, who looked up at her, prepared for beating or caress, like spaniels, appealed to a mass of emotions, and they were not all of them bad. What such women wanted, she saw, was to be told that they were parts of a whole, as a fly in a milk jug seeks the support of a spoon. She knew further that one must have a motive in order to work; she was strong enough to convince; and power, which should have been hers as a mother, was dear to her even when it came by illegitimate means. Another gift was hers, without which the rest had been useless; she could take flights into obscurity. After telling people what to do, she gave them, in a whisper at first, later in a voice that lapsed and quavered, some mystic reasons why. She could only discover them by peeping, as it were, over the rim of the world; and to begin with she tried honestly to say no more than she saw there. The present state, where one is bound down, a target for pigmy arrows, seemed to her for the most part dull, and sometimes intolerable. Some draught, vague and sweet as chloroform, which confused out-lines and made daily life dance before the eyes with hints of a vista beyond, was what they needed, and nature had fitted her to give it them. 'Life was a hard school,' she said, 'How could one bear it unless –' and then there came a rhapsody about trees and flowers and fishes in the deep, and an eternal harmony, with her head back, and her eyes half shut, to see better. 'We felt often that we had a Sibyl among us,' writes Miss Haig; and if Sibyls are only half inspired, conscious of the folly of their disciples, sorry for them, very vain of their applause and much muddled in their own brains all at once, then Miss Willatt was a Sibyl too. But the most striking part of the picture is the unhappy view that it gives of the spiritual state of Bloomsbury at this period – when Miss Willatt brooded in Woburn Square like some gorged spider at the centre of her web, and all along the filaments unhappy women came running, slight hen-like figures, frightened by the sun and the carts and the dreadful world, and longing to hide themselves from the entire panorama in the shade of Miss Willatt's skirts. The Andrews, the Spaldings, young Mr Charles Jenkinson 'who has since left us', old Lady Battersby, who suffered from the gout, Miss Cecily Haig, Ebenezer Umphelby who knew more about beetles than anyone in Europe – all these people who dropped into tea and had Sunday supper and conversation afterwards, come to life again, and tempt us almost intolerably to know more about them. What did they look like, and do, what did they want from Miss Willatt and what did they think of her, in private? – but we shall never know, or hear of them again. They have been rolled into the earth irrecoverably.

Indeed there is only space left to give the pith of that last long chapter, which Miss Linsett called 'Fulfilment'. Certainly, it is one of the strangest. Miss Linsett who was powerfully fascinated by the idea of death, coos and preens herself in his presence and can hardly bring herself to make an end. It is easier to write about death, which is common, than about a single life; there are general statements which one likes to use once in a way for oneself, and there is something in saying good-bye to a person which leads to smooth manners and pleasant sensations. Moreover, Miss Linsett had a natural distrust of life, which was boisterous and commonplace, and had never treated her too well, and took every opportunity of proving that human beings die, as though she snubbed some ill-mannered schoolboy. If one wished it thus, one could give more details of those last months of Miss Willatt's life than of any that have gone before. We know precisely what she died of. The narrative slackens to a funeral pace and every word of it is relished; but in truth, it amounts to little more than this. Miss Willatt had suffered from an internal complaint for some years, but mentioned it only to her intimate friends. Then, in the autumn of 1884, she caught a chill. 'It was the beginning of the end, and from that date we had little hope.' They told her, once, that she was dying, but she 'seemed absorbed in a mat which she was working for her nephew'. When she took to her bed she did not ask to see anyone, save her old servant Emma Grice who had been with her for thirty years. At length, on the night of the 18th of October, 'a stormy autumn night, with flying clouds and gusts of rain', Miss Linsett was summoned to say good-bye. Miss Willatt was lying on her back, with her eyes shut, and her head which was half in shadow looked 'very grand'. Miss Willatt lay thus all night long without speaking or turning or opening her eyes. Once she raised her left hand, 'upon which she wore her mother's wedding ring', and let it fall again; they expected something more, but not knowing what she wanted they did nothing, and half an hour later the counterpane lay still, and they crept from their corners, seeing that she was dead.

After reading this scene, with its accompaniment of inappropriate detail, its random flourishes whipping up a climax – how she changed colour, and they rubbed her forehead with eau-de-cologne, how Mr Sully called and went away again, how creepers tapped on the window, how the room grew pale as the dawn rose, how sparrows twittered and carts began to rattle through the square to market – one sees that Miss Linsett liked death because it gave her an emotion, and made her feel things for the time as though they meant something. For the moment she loved Miss Willatt; Miss Willatt's death the moment after made her even happy. It was an end undisturbed by the chance of a fresh beginning. But afterwards, when she went home and had her breakfast, she felt lonely, for they had been in the habit of going to Kew Gardens together on Sundays.

Notes

1. Anatole France, pseudonym of Jacques Anatole François Thibault (1844–1924), French writer; Walter Pater (1839–94), critic and essayist.
2. Lord Mayo, the Viceroy of India, was assassinated on 8th February 1872.
3. George Romney (1734–1802), portrait painter.
4. In her notes for *The Complete Shorter Fiction of Virginia Woolf*, Susan Dick points out that if Virginia Woolf had revised this story, she would no doubt have corrected the inconsistencies in the dates mentioned.
5. Mount Pentelicus was famous for its marble, which was used in the construction of the Acropolis; Pheidias was an ancient Greek sculptor (fl. *c*.490–430 BC), who towards the end of his life was imprisoned and possibly exiled following accusations from his enemies.
6. Theocritus (*c*.310–250 BC), Greek pastoral poet.
7. Thomas Love Peacock (1785–1866), writer.
8. Play by Sophocles (*c*.496–406 BC).
9. Virginia Woolf's brackets.
10. William Wordsworth, 'Lines Composed a Few Miles Above Tintern Abbey' (1798).
11. Series of novels by Sir Walter Scott (1771–1832).
12. Harriet Martineau (1802–76), social, economic and historical writer.

Biographical note

Adeline Virginia Stephen was born in London on 25th January 1882, the third of four children of Leslie Stephen, a distinguished man of letters, and Julia Jackson Duckworth, a widow. Both her parents had children from previous marriages, and she grew up in a large active family, which spent long summer holidays in St Ives. Educated at home, she had unlimited access to her father's library; she always intended to be a writer.

In 1895, her mother died unexpectedly, and soon after this Virginia suffered her first nervous breakdown; she was to be beset by periods of mental illness throughout her life. Following the death of their father in 1904, the four orphaned Stephens moved to Bloomsbury, where their home became the centre of what came to be known as the Bloomsbury Group. This circle included Clive Bell (whom Virginia's sister Vanessa married in 1907), Lytton Strachey, John Maynard Keynes and Leonard Woolf, whom Virginia was to marry in 1912, after his return from seven years' public service in Ceylon.

Virginia completed her first novel, *The Voyage Out*, in 1913, but her subsequent severe breakdown delayed its publication until 1915, by which time the Woolfs had settled at Hogarth House in Richmond. As a therapeutic hobby for Virginia, they bought a small hand press, on which they set and printed several short works by themselves and their friends. The first publication of The Hogarth Press appeared in 1917, and thereafter it gradually developed into a considerable enterprise, at first publishing works by then relatively unknown writers, such as T.S. Eliot, Katherine Mansfield and E.M. Forster, as well as the Woolfs themselves.

While living at Richmond, Virginia wrote her second, rather orthodox novel, *Night and Day* (1919), but was concurrently composing more experimental pieces such as *Kew Gardens*

(1919) and *Monday or Tuesday* (1921). In 1920 the Woolfs bought Monk's House in Rodmell, and there Virginia began her third novel, *Jacob's Room* (1922). This was followed by *Mrs Dalloway* (1925), *To the Lighthouse* (1927) and *The Waves* (1931), and these three novels established her as one of the leading writers of the Modernist movement. *Orlando*, a highly imaginative 'biography' inspired by her involvement with Vita Sackville-West, was published in 1928.

The Years appeared in 1937, and she had more or less completed her final novel, *Between the Acts*, when, unable to face another attack of mental illness, she drowned herself in the River Ouse on 28th March 1941.

SELECTED TITLES FROM HESPERUS PRESS

Author	Title	Foreword writer
Mikhail Bulgakov	*A Dog's Heart*	A.S. Byatt
Mikhail Bulgakov	*The Fatal Eggs*	Doris Lessing
Anthony Burgess	*The Eve of St Venus*	
Colette	*Claudine's House*	Doris Lessing
Marie Ferranti	*The Princess of Mantua*	
Beppe Fenoglio	*A Private Affair*	Paul Bailey
F. Scott Fitzgerald	*The Popular Girl*	Helen Dunmore
F. Scott Fitzgerald	*The Rich Boy*	John Updike
Graham Greene	*No Man's Land*	David Lodge
Franz Kafka	*Metamorphosis*	Martin Jarvis
Franz Kafka	*The Trial*	Zadie Smith
D.H. Lawrence	*Wintry Peacock*	Amit Chaudhuri
Rosamond Lehmann	*The Gipsy's Baby*	Niall Griffiths
Carlo Levi	*Words are Stones*	Anita Desai
André Malraux	*The Way of the Kings*	Rachel Seiffert
Katherine Mansfield	*In a German Pension*	Linda Grant
Katherine Mansfield	*Prelude*	William Boyd
Vladimir Mayakovsky	*My Discovery of America*	Colum McCann
Luigi Pirandello	*Loveless Love*	
Françoise Sagan	*The Unmade Bed*	
Jean-Paul Sartre	*The Wall*	Justin Cartwright
George Bernard Shaw	*The Adventures of the Black Girl in Her Search for God*	Colm Tóibín
Georges Simenon	*Three Crimes*	
Leonard Woolf	*A Tale Told by Moonlight*	Victoria Glendinning